T0302727

SESSIONS:
Eric Clapton

Andrew Wild

SONICBOND

sonicbondpublishing.com

Sonicbond Publishing Limited
www.sonicbondpublishing.co.uk
Email: info@sonicbondpublishing.co.uk

First Published in the United Kingdom 2022
First Published in the United States 2022

British Library Cataloguing in Publication Data:
A Catalogue record for this book is available from the British Library

ISBN 978-1-78952-177-1

Typeset in ITC Garamond & ITC Avant Garde
Printed and bound in England

Graphic design and typesetting: Full Moon Media

SESSIONS:
Eric Clapton

Andrew Wild

SONICBOND

sonicbondpublishing.com

Acknowledgements

Thank you: Damian Haigh, Marc Roberty, Emma Spires, John Hamilton, Tim Renwick, Rosie Wild (who provided a single word), Agathe Fourie, Stephen Lambe, Mark Lewisohn, the editors of *Where's Eric?* and Ross at The Squire Presents (*thesquirepresents.co.uk*).

Unless noted otherwise, all Eric Clapton quotations are taken from *Eric Clapton: The Autobiography*. Unless noted otherwise, all George Harrison and John Lennon quotations are taken from The Beatles' *Anthology*. Unless noted otherwise, all Glyn Johns quotations are taken from *Sound Man : A Life Recording Hits with the Rolling Stones, The Who, Led Zeppelin, The Eagles, Eric Clapton, The Faces*. Unless noted otherwise all Bobby Whitlock quotattions are from *A Rock 'n' Roll Autobiography*. Unless noted otherwise, all Phil Collins quotations are from *Not Dead Yet: The Autobiography*. See bibliography for full details.

For Amanada, Rosie and Amy. And for Eric of course.

Also by Andrew Wild

Local history

108 Steps Around Macclesfield (Sigma Press, 1994 / 2nd edition, Rumble Strips, 2018)
Exploring Chester (Sigma Press, 1996 / re-publication, Rumble Strips, 2018)
Ever Forward (MADS, 1997)

Biographies

Play On (Twelfth Night, 2009)
One for the Record (Avalon, 2013 / 2nd edition, 2018)

Music

Pink Floyd Song by Song (Fonthill, 2017)
Queen ... On Track (Sonicbond, 2018)
The Beatles: An A-Z Guide to Every Song: On Track (Sonicbond, 2019)
Solo Beatles 1969-1980 ... On Track (Sonicbond, 2020)
Crosby, Stills & Nash ... On Track (Sonicbond, 2020)
Dire Straits ... On Track (Sonicbond, 2021)
Fleetwood Mac in the 1970s (Sonicbond, 2021)
Eric Clapton: Solo ... On Track (Sonicbond, 2021)

Films

James Bond ... On Screen (Sonicbond, 2021)

Plays

The Difficult Crossing (Stagescripts, 2016)
A Difficult Man (Rumble Strips, 2021)

SESSIONS:
Eric Clapton

Contents

Introduction

Assessing the career of one of the most productive artists of his generation is a challenge.

From his first releases as a member of the Yardbirds in the 1960s through to the 2020s, Eric Clapton has released over fifty studio and live albums as a solo artist or as a full-time member of The Yardbirds, John Mayall's Bluesbreakers, Cream, Blind Faith and Derek and the Dominos.

In addition to these, Clapton has contributed to close to over four hundred songs by friends, colleagues, ex-bandmembers and peers – sometimes he has provided just a trademark guitar solo on a single track; elsewhere, with, say *All Things Must Pass*, *Lost In Austin, The Pros and Cons of Hitchhiking* or *How To Become Clairvoyant*, he has been an integral part of an entire album.

Eric Clapton has played with the very famous, the obscure and the unexpected: Bob Dylan, Aretha Franklin, The Rolling Stones, Sting, Phil Collins, Rod Stewart, all four of the Beatles, Martha Veléz, Jonathan Kelly, Corey Hart, Stephen Bishop, Hawkwind, Ray Charles, Kate Bush, The Tony Rich Project, Toots and the Maytals, Mary J. Blige.

Over the last thirty-five years or so, I have collected, as far as I know, all of the two hundred sessions on which Clapton has played as a guest artist, initiated by his astounding performance on Roger Waters' *The Pros And Cons Of Hitch-Hiking*. This has been an illuminating, enlightening and occasionally expensive process. No thanks here to Robbie Robertson, formerly of The Band, who released a demo featuring Clapton on a limited edition (read: expensive) hand-signed box set.

This book puts these into context across nearly six decades of sessions. If you've never listened to 'Beat Of The Night', 'Sexual Revolution', 'Annie', 'Cloud Nine', 'I Wish It Would Rain Down', 'Wonderful World', 'Ships In The Night', 'Madame X', 'Don't Worry Kyoko (Mummy's Only Looking for Her Hand in the Snow)', 'Barcelona', 'Give Me Back My Dynamite', 'Never Without You' and 'Dirty City' then these, and many others, are worth tracking down.

If his own albums are the main story, then these recordings run alongside: an alternative history of one of rock's most prolific musicians.

Andrew Wild
Rainow, 2022

What constitutes a 'session'?

In this context, a session (and an entry in this book) means a song that Eric Clapton has played and/or sung on a studio or live album by another artist, he is not credited as the primary artist for the release, and it has been commercially released on vinyl, CD or download.

For example, he plays on every track on Marc Benno's *Lost In Austin*, but the album is credited solely to Benno.

Conversely, if Eric is officially co-credited on an album or single, then these fall outside the remit of this book: joint collaborations with Delaney and Bonnie (*On Tour*), Steve Winwood (*Live From Madison Square Garden*), JJ Cale (*The Road To Escondido*), B.B. King (*Riding With The King*), Wynton Marsalis (*Play The Blues : Live from Jazz at Lincoln Center*), Elton John ('Runaway Train'), Sting ('It's Probably Me)', Randy Crawford ('Knocking On Heaven's Door') and a few others are omitted. Likewise, Clapton was a member of the Yardbirds for *Sonny Boy Williamson and the Yardbirds* and was a key member of the short-lived studio band The Powerhouse. These are all considered here as part of his regular discography, not as sessions for others.

Just to confuse matters, I have included Hiroshi Fujiwari's *Cappuccino* EP, despite Eric's co-credit, as this collaboration was only released in Japan.

In some cases, sessions will be mentioned for which Eric has been credited in the past but can now be disproven: 'New Day' by Jackie Lomax, for example. There are also some entries where Eric's involvement is in doubt (or unconfirmed), for example, *One For The Boys*, *Legalize It!*, and 'The Intro And The Outro'. There is also Françoise Hardy's 'Contre Vents et Marées': Eric is not credited here, but we put forward a case that he does indeed play on this track from 1998. We will also highlight some deliberately false credits, such as 'Bye Bye Love' and *Ham Strangled Bastard,* as well as some unreleased sessions.

Tread carefully: where necessary, the text will advise caution.

Congratulations if you've collected them all. Let's have a pint when time allows.

The 1960s

Eric Clapton, at heart, is a blues singer. He's also one of the best guitarists of his generation. Since the mid-sixties, there has been a real cachet to having Clapton perform on an album, and he seems to have turned down very few opportunities to add his distinctive playing to anyone who asked him.

But in 1963-1964, the shoe was on the other foot. Eric was the padawan at the feet of the masters, recording a live album with American singer Sonny Boy Williamson and performing sessions for touring musician Otis Spann with his boss Muddy Waters.

Clapton was a few weeks past his nineteenth birthday.

As the decade progressed, and as Clapton moved from the Yardbirds to John Mayall's Bluesbreakers to Cream, the opportunities for sessions were slim. But with Cream growing apart in mid-1968 Clapton was able to devote much more time to playing with others.

In the three years between the last-but-one Cream tour, which ended in June 1968, though to his self-imposed exile from recording after abortive sessions with Derek and the Dominoes in April-May 1971, he played on over thirty albums for other musicians. His session work here is both considerable and impressive.

Otis Spann: 'Stirs Me Up' (single) / *Raw Blues*

Recorded May 1964 at Decca Studios, West Hampstead, London.
'Stirs Me Up' released as a single a-side, September 1964. Did not chart. ***Raw Blues*** released 1967. Did not chart. Produced by Mike Vernon.

'Stirs Me Up' (Spann)
'Pretty Girls Everywhere' (Church, Williams)

Otis Spann was a leading post-war Chicago blues pianist. He replaced Maceo Merriweather as Muddy Waters' piano player in late 1952 and was touring the UK with Waters when producer Mike Vernon recorded two songs at Decca Studios in London. Eric:

> Mike Vernon, who owned Blue Horizon records, asked me to go down to a studio to do some session work, and I found myself playing with Muddy Waters and Otis Spann, two of my all-time heroes. I was absolutely terrified, but not because I felt that I couldn't carry my weight musically. I just didn't know how to behave around these guys.

Spann's 'Stirs Me Up' would be released as a single. Clapton plays some fluid guitar lines. Ransom Knowling plays bass, Willie 'Big Eyes' Smith is on drums and Muddy Waters plays guitar. There is an uncredited harmonica which some sources claim is Jimmy Page, overdubbed at a later session. These same musicians play on a version of Eugene Church's 'Pretty Girls Everywhere'.

This song would not be released until 1967 on the compilation album *Raw Blues*. Eric:

> We cut a song called 'Pretty Girls Everywhere I Go', and I played lead over Muddy's rhythm while Otis sang and played piano. I was in heaven, and they seemed pretty happy with what I did.

Champion Jack Dupree: *From New Orleans To Chicago*

Recorded February 1966 at Wessex Studios, London. Released April 1966. Did not chart. Produced by Mike Vernon.

'Third Degree' (Boyd, Dixon)
'Shim-Sham-Shimmy' (Bobby and Danny Robinson)
'Calcutta Blues' (Dupree)

It would be almost two years before Eric played his next session, again for producer Mike Vernon. Vernon recorded several albums with blues pianist Champion Jack Dupree, providing a band for these three tracks consisting of Eric Clapton, his boss John Mayall on harmonica, Malcolm Pool and Keef Hartley from The Artwoods on bass and drums and Tony McPhee of The Groundhogs on guitar.

'Third Degree' is a burning 6/8 blues, dominated by Dupree's authoritative vocal and Mayall's harmonica. Eric drops a skittish, heavily reverbed solo, although this version can't hold a candle to Eddie Boyd's 1953 original. Clapton would record a mighty take of the song himself almost thirty years later on his 1994 blues album *From The Cradle*.

'Shim-Sham-Shimmy' is a reworking of an earlier single by Dupree. The band enter hesitantly but then begin to cook, with brilliant solos by Clapton and Mayall. Dupree expresses his delight.

'Calcutta Blues' from these same sessions would be released on the 1967 compilation album *Raw Blues*. This slow blues is the real deal – trilling piano, wailing harmonica, Eric's fluid guitar licks and a strong vocal performance.

Bob Dylan: 'If You Gotta Go, Go Now'

Recorded 12 May 1965 at Levy's Recording Studios, London. Unreleased. Produced by Tom Wilson.

'If You Gotta Go, Go Now' (Dylan)

Eric Clapton's first recording session with Bob Dylan did not go well.

Dylan was in the UK for an eight-date concert tour between 30 April and 10 May. This was documented in the film *Don't Look Back*. One intriguing scene shows Bob Dylan in a hotel room watching John Mayall's Bluesbreakers on television: they appeared live on ITV's *Ollie & Fred's Five O'clock Club* on 4 May 1965. Dylan completed his tour with two shows at The Royal Albert Hall (9 and 10 May) and, a few days later, spent the afternoon at Levy's Recording

Studio in London. This was used to record promo spots for Columbia but also included some sessions with The Bluesbreakers. Eric:

> It was just a jam session. He was interested in John Mayall. John had recorded a song called 'Crawling Up A Hill' and that interested Bob. I was just the guitar player on the session. I didn't actually speak to Bob at this time. He never came and actually spoke. I just watched him. We played for two hours. The next thing I knew, he was gone.

Only one song has been heard: a rough-and-ready ninety-second take of 'If You Gotta Go, Go Now'. When Dylan messes up the count-in, someone starts laughing and says, 'You haven't worked much with bands, have you?' Dylan responds with, 'I don't need no count, man.' Only Dylan's piano and Hughie Flint's drums are audible: it seems that no-one else is playing.

A complete version of 'If You Gotta Go, Go Now' has not emerged from the session, nor any of the jams that Eric mentions. The session was not included in the 2015 eighteen-disc box *The Bootleg Series Vol. 12: The Cutting Edge 1965–1966,* which otherwise includes every Dylan studio session from January 1965 through to March 1966.

The Who Orchestra: 'Waltz For A Pig'

Recorded early 1966. Released March 1966 (UK), April 1966 (US). Highest chart position: UK: 5; US did not chart. Producer unknown.

'Waltz For A Pig' (Baker)

'Waltz For A Pig' was the b-side of The Who's single 'Substitute', credited to The Who Orchestra, but actually performed by the British R & B band The Graham Bond Organisation. This plodding, horn-driven instrumental was written by the band's drummer, Ginger Baker, soon to join Cream. Some sources credit Eric on this track, but this seems improbable, and aural evidence is inconclusive. File this under 'unlikely'.

Caroline Munro: 'Tar and Cement' / 'The Sporting Life'

Recorded 1967 at E.M.I. Studios, Abbey Road, London. Released May 1967. Highest position: Did not chart. Produced by Mark Wirtz.

'Tar And Cement' (Vance, Pockriss, Celentano, Beretta, Del Prete)
'The Sporting Life [Sporting Life Blues]' (McGhee)

In 1967, Caroline Munro had yet to turn many young men's heads as the voluptuous model on the Lamb's Navy Rum adverts. Her debut single, 'Tar and Cement' is a reworking of the Adriano Celentano song 'Il Ragazzo Della Via Gluck'. Around the same time, producer Mark Wirtz, who was contracted to E.M.I., had recorded Tomorrow's 'My White Bicycle' and Keith West's 'Excerpt From A Teenage Opera'. 'Tar And Cement' would be released on the E.M.I. subsidiary Columbia.

According to many online sources, the musicians on 'Tar and Cement' are Eric Clapton, Jack Bruce, Ginger Baker and Tomorrow's Steve Howe. This seems unlikely: the arrangement is lush with strings and horns, and there is little evidence of Cream as a backing band here. In particular, the rigid drumming style owes nothing to Ginger Baker, and although there are a few bluesy guitar licks, they don't sound like Eric's style at all.

The b-side is a version of Brownie McGhee's 'Sporting Life Blues', although the single credits Peter Eden and Mark Wirtz as writers. Munro, speaking to *The Guardian* in 2019:

> I was only sixteen, just out of convent school, when I sang that. It was ridiculous, really. I didn't know anything about living a sporting life.

Despite Munro's unconvincing vocals, the backing is pure mid-sixties R & B. There are some distinctive Clapton guitar licks and a second guitarist, which we can assume is Howe. It, therefore, seems likely that Bruce and Baker are the rhythm section. Munro would go on to a successful career as eye candy in films including *The Abominable Dr. Phibes* (1971), *The Golden Voyage of Sinbad* (1974), *At the Earth's Core* (1976) and *The Spy Who Loved Me* (1977).

Bonzo Dog Doo-Dah Band: *Gorilla*

Recorded 1967. Released October 1967. Highest position: Did not chart. Produced by Gerry Bron, Lyn Birkbeck.

'The Intro and the Outro' (Stanshall)

The Bonzo Dog Doo-Dah Band were unique: a comedy band that could really play and were actually funny. Their five albums released between 1967 and 1972 are highly recommended.

'The Intro and the Outro' from their debut, *Gorilla*, is a sublime spoof of the introduction of instrumentalists soloing in a jazz band, as chief Bonzo Viv Stanshall announces each member of the Bonzos (and what they play), followed by a long list of clever jokes – such as Charles de Gaulle 'on accordion', Adolf Hitler 'looking very relaxed on vibes' and The Incredible Shrinking Man supposedly playing the enormous euphonium. This song still raises a smile after many listens.

Eric Clapton is credited for playing ukulele, which I believe is just a wry joke on his then-status as the world's most famous guitar player. According to Stanshall's monologue, the Bonzos themselves play the following instruments on the recording: 'Legs' Larry Smith on drums, Sam Spoons on rhythm pole, Vernon Dudley Bohay-Nowell on bass guitar, Neil Innes on piano, Rodney Slater on alto saxophone, Roger Ruskin Spear on tenor saxophone and Vivian Stanshall on trumpet. This continues, introducing 'over there, Eric Clapton on ukulele. Hi Eric!'. Smith and Clapton were friends and some sources suggest that Clapton does, indeed, perform on this song. This observer doubts that assertion, but it has been reported, without proof, in several sources. We'll include it here, just in case.

Also mentioned on the recording, and are also unlikely to have actually performed, are: John Wayne on xylophone, Robert Morley on guitar, Billy Butlin on spoons, Princess Anne on sousaphone, Liberace on clarinet, Garner Ted Armstrong on vocals, Lord Snooty and his Pals (tap dancing), Harold Wilson on violin, Franklyn MacCormack on harmonica, Sir Kenneth Clark on bass saxophone, a session gorilla ('vox humana'), The Incredible Shrinking Man on euphonium, Peter Scott on duck call, Casanova ('horn'), General Charles de Gaulle on accordion, Roy Rogers on Trigger, Wild Man of Borneo on bongos, the entire Count Basie Orchestra on triangle, The Rawlinsons on trombone, Dan Druff on harp, Quasimodo on bells, Brainiac on banjo, Val Doonican ('as himself' – 'hello there!'), Max Jaffa ('very appealing'), Zebra Kid and Horace Batchelor on percussion and J. Arthur Rank on gong.

Aretha Franklin: *Lady Soul*

Recorded September 1967 at Atlantic Studios, New York. Released January 1968. Highest position: US: 2, UK: did not chart. Produced by Jerry Wexler.

'Good To Me As I Am To You' (Franklin, White)
Two words: Aretha Franklin. 'Good To Me As I Am To You' represents Eric Clapton's first American guest recording session, recorded in the same studios (and in the same time frame) as Cream's *Wheels of Fire*. 'Good To Me As I Am To You' is a quite brilliant soul/gospel song from one of the greatest voices of the twentieth century. It comes from the same album as the classics '(You Make Me Feel Like) A Natural Woman' and 'Chain of Fools'. Eric does his best B.B. King fills, but he's mixed low and doesn't get a chance to shine – but then who wants to complete with Aretha's peerless singing?

The Mothers Of Invention: *We're Only In It For The Money*

Recorded March–October 1967 at Capitol Studios, Los Angeles; Mayfair Studios and Apostolic Studios, New York City. Released March 1968. Highest position: US: 30, UK did not chart. Produced by Frank Zappa.

'Are You Hung Up?' (Zappa)
'Nasal Retentive Calliope Music' (Zappa)
There's no doubt that Frank Zappa was a true original. With his band The Mothers Of Invention (1964-1975) and as part of his parallel solo career from 1967, he released sixty uncompromising albums in a witty and musical adventurous style that was all his own. Another fifty albums have followed posthumously since his death in 1993, aged 52.

We're Only In It For The Money, The Mothers' third album, is a biting satire of left-wing and right-wing politics. Although Eric Clapton appears on two songs, this is not an Eric Clapton session *per se*. 'Are You Hung Up?' is a short montage of dialogue and musique concrete. Clapton can be heard saying, 'Uh, out of sight. Are, are you hung up?' to an unknown correspondent. 'Nasal Retentive Calliope Music', which opens side two, sounds like a dry run for 'Revolution #9'. Clapton utters 'Beautiful! God! It's God! I see God!' twenty-three seconds in.

It's been reported that Eric also appears in a similar fashion on *Lumpy Gravy*, recorded simultaneously with *We're Only In It For The Money*. Zappa dismissed this in a later interview.

George Harrison: *Wonderwall Music*

Recorded December 1967 – January 1968 at Kingsway Studios, London, and E.M.I. Studios, Abbey Road, London. Released November 1968. Highest position: US: 49, UK: did not chart. Produced by George Harrison.

'Ski-ing' (Harrison)

And thus starts one of the great soap operas of the 1960s and 1970s.

Eric Clapton first met George Harrison in December 1964 when The Yardbirds were one of the support acts on *Another Beatles Christmas Show*, a three-week, twice-a-night season at the Hammersmith Odeon. This featured music, pantomime sketches and comedy. Eric:

> Even though we were quite low on the bill, playing these shows was fine for us. All our followers from the Crawdaddy would come and see us, so we had our own fans to play to, and they actually listened to our music. It was different for the Beatles. One night I went to the back of the auditorium to watch them, and you couldn't hear the music at all because of the screaming. Hanging out backstage at the Odeon was where I had my first meeting with the Beatles. George and I hit it off right away. He seemed to like what I did, and we talked shop a lot. He showed me his collection of Gretsch guitars, and I showed him my light-gauge strings, which I always bought from a shop on Earlham Street. I gave him some, and this was the start of what was to eventually become a long friendship.

Three years later, George was asked to provide the soundtrack to *Wonderwall*, an odd film that centres around a would-be voyeur who sees a psychedelic fantasy land through a hole in the wall of his bedsit. George is composer and producer – he neither plays nor sings, preferring to employ Liverpool band The Remo Four and some Indian session musicians recorded in Bombay.

Eric plays on one song. 'Ski-ing' is little more than a powerful, repetitive blues riff with a freaky Indian backdrop. It's very much of its time and probably sounded dated even in 1968.

Wonderwall Music was the first solo album by a member of the Beatles and Eric is credited as 'Eddie Clayton', just as George would be given the pseudonym 'L'Angelo Misterioso' when he added rhythm guitar to Cream's 'Badge' in October 1968. Eric would go on to play on three other albums by George Harrison: *All Things Must Pass* (1970), *George Harrison* (1979) and

Cloud Nine (1987), as well as on solo material by the other three ex-Beatles.
And marry George's wife. But that's another story.

Jackie Lomax: *Is This What You Want?*

Recorded June 1968 at Trident Studios, London. Released March 1969. Highest position: US: 145, UK did not chart. Produced by George Harrison.

'Sour Milk Sea' (Harrison)
'The Eagle Laughs At You' (Lomax)
'You've Got Me Thinking' (Lomax)

By mid-1968, Eric Clapton began to feel hemmed in by the limitations of the three-piece Cream. Wanting to work with new people, he donated his skills to more than twenty sessions for other artists over the next two and a half years. This gives the collector a rich seam of interesting music to explore.

Singer, guitarist and Jackie Lomax had been part of the early sixties Merseybeat scene as the singer of The Undertakers. They released four singles for Pye in 1963-1964; the third, 'Just a Little Bit', managed one week on the Top 50 in the UK Singles Chart in April 1964. Lomax was later signed as a solo artist to Apple Records and George Harrison produced the album *Is This What You Want?* in London and Los Angeles. Three of the London tracks include Eric Clapton on lead guitar, along with Nicky Hopkins (piano), Klaus Voormann (bass), Ringo Starr (drums) and Harrison himself.

'Sour Milk Sea' was demoed by Harrison for The Beatles in May 1968. Lomax' version recorded the following month deserved to be a huge hit. It rocks hard with a strong vocal and some stinging Cream-style lead guitar.

'The Eagle Laughs At You' is a 1968 take on the Bo Diddley beat, with a heavily-distorted sound. Clapton's contribution is limited to some grunting guitar stabs. 'You've Got Me Thinking' is soulful rock, with horns and backing singers and some bluesy licks from Eric.

Lomax recorded the single 'New Day' in March–April 1969. Clapton has long been credited as taking part but guitarist Tim Renwick, who played on the session, confirmed to the author that 'Mr. C' did not attend.

Martha Veléz: *Fiends & Angels*

Recorded June-July 1968 at Decca Studios, West Hampstead. Released 1969. Did not chart. Produced by Mike Vernon.

'It Takes A Lot To Laugh, It Takes A Train To Cry' (Dylan)
'I'm Gonna Leave You' (Johnson, Whitfield)
'Feel So Bad' (Hopkins)
'In My Girlish Days' (Lawler)

American singer Martha Veléz came from a musical theatre background, joining the Broadway cast of *Hair* in April 1968. She came to the attention of Seymour

Stein and Richard Gotterher, the founders of Sire Records. They recorded some demos and sent her to London to work with Mike Vernon, who had produced several hit albums for Decca and his own Blue Horizon, including *Bluesbreakers With Eric Clapton*. In a remarkable six-month period, Vernon had produced the debut albums by Savoy Brown, Ten Years After, David Bowie, Chicken Shack and Fleetwood Mac. Vernon recruited Eric Clapton, Stan Webb and Christine Perfect from these projects to work with Martha Veléz. Jack Bruce of Cream and Mitch Mitchell of The Jimi Hendrix Experience also contributed. Veléz in *Ethnomusicology Review* in 2015:

> Working on that first album was very intimidating. I'd walk in and there would be all these people. They were at the top of their game in that era, and I had not really done this music to that extent – I hadn't worked it, hadn't been on the road with it, I hadn't done anything but really have a fire for it. We were working in the Decca Studios, and at that time, it was set up for orchestras: bleacher-style, where the instrumentalists would sit with the conductor standing on the floor level. It was perfect for me in a way because I was used to performing on a stage, and standing on the top section this was like standing on a stage. We'd just arrange things as if we just started playing and just didn't stop: nobody sat down and wrote out specifics for the basic track arrangements. That wasn't as important to me as really finding the groove with these artists.

The four tracks on which Eric plays are basic, powerful blues-rock. Dylan's 'It Takes A Lot To Laugh, It Takes A Train To Cry' sticks close to the original, with a soft, reflective lead vocal and two tight guitar solos. 'In My Girlish Days' is a mid-paced twelve-bar with a very loud guitar solo. Veléz belts the vocal at the top of her range. 'Feel So Bad' pairs Martha's powerful vocals with a gritty harmonica, loud guitar and bubbling bass. The guitar solo is heavily overdriven and pure Cream-era Clapton. 'I'm Gonna Leave You' is a dominated by Clapton's constant lead guitar riffing. The solo is by an uncredited harmonica player (perhaps Jack Bruce) and the song finishes as a lively free for all.

The Beatles: *The Beatles*

Recorded September 1968 at E.M.I. Studios, Abbey Road, London. ***The Beatles*** released November 1968. Highest position: US: 1, UK: 1. Produced by George Martin. ***Love*** released November 2006. Highest position: US: 4, UK: 3. Produced by George Martin and Giles Martin.

'While My Guitar Gently Weeps' (Harrison)
'Lady Madonna (Love version)' (Lennon, McCartney)
By September 1968, The Beatles had been recording their ninth album for four months. Tempers were frayed. George's first contribution to the sessions was his

song 'Not Guilty', which took over one hundred takes to perfect and was still left in the can. His second was the classic 'While My Guitar Gently Weeps'. George:

> I wrote 'While My Guitar Gently Weeps' at my mother's house in Warrington. I was thinking about the Chinese *I Ching,* the Book of Changes... The Eastern concept is that whatever happens is all meant to be, and that there's no such thing as coincidence – every little item that's going down has a purpose. 'While My Guitar Gently Weeps' was a simple study based on that theory. I decided to write a song based on the first thing I saw upon opening any book – as it would be a relative to that moment, at that time. I picked up a book at random, opened it, saw 'gently weeps', then laid the book down again and started the song.

After recording a couple of demo takes, the first formal session was on 16 August 1968. Fourteen takes were recorded but the magic wasn't there. George speaking to *Guitar Player* in 1987:

> I worked on that song with John, Paul, and Ringo one day, and they were not interested in it at all. And I knew inside of me that it was a nice song.

Despite overdubs over two sessions in early September, George was still not satisfied as he told *Guitar Player*:

> The next day [5 September 1968], I was with Eric, and I was going into the session, and I said, 'We're going to do this song. Come on and play on it'. He said, 'Oh, no. I can't do that. Nobody ever plays on the Beatles records'. I said, 'Look, it's my song, and I want you to play on it'. So Eric came in, and the other guys were as good as gold because he was there. It left me free to just play the rhythm and do the vocal.

The basic track was George Harrison (acoustic guitar, vocals), Paul McCartney (piano, organ), Ringo Starr (drums) and Eric Clapton (electric guitar). Eric:

> George drove me over to Abbey Road Studios, where he was recording. When we arrived, he told me they were going to record one of his songs and asked me to play guitar on it. I was flattered, thinking that not many people get asked to play on a Beatles record. The song was 'While My Guitar Gently Weeps'. We did just one take.

Eric's memory is faulty here. He played on the majority of twenty-eight takes (numbered 17 to 45). Take 27 was released in 2018 and is very clearly a different version. The next day, Paul overdubbed bass guitar and background vocals to complete the recording. Eric:

> I thought it sounded fantastic.

It did. And it still does.

The 2006 remix /mash-up album *Love* edits a short section of Eric's solo into 'Lady Madonna', where it feels totally out of place.

The Dirty Mac: *The Rolling Stones' Rock & Roll Circus*

Recorded December 1968 at Intertel (V.T.R. Services) Studio, Wycombe Road, Wembley. Released October 1996. Highest position: US: 92, UK did not chart. Deluxe edition released 2019. Produced by Jimmy Miller.

'Yer Blues' (Lennon, McCartney)
'Whole Lotta Yoko' (Ono)
'Warmup Jam' (Lennon, Clapton, Mitchell, Richards)
'Revolution' (Lennon, McCartney)
'Yer Blues (take 2)' (Lennon, McCartney)

In December 1968, John Lennon took part in a filmed event arranged by The Rolling Stones, centred around a circus theme. The Stones were joined by a number of guests, including Lennon, who formed a one-off band called The Dirty Mac with Keith Richards (bass), Mitch Mitchell (drums) and Eric Clapton (lead guitar). Cream had performed their farewell concerts two weeks beforehand. It was the first time Lennon had performed without Paul McCartney by his side since 1957

Displeased with their performance, The Rolling Stones shelved the project. The original film stock was thought to be lost or destroyed, but parts were found in Stones' alumnus Ian Stewart's belongings following his death in 1985 and more was rediscovered in The Who's vault in London in 1993. A new mix and edit for commercial release was completed in 1996 and premiered at the New York Film Festival.

The accompanying CD presented six songs by The Rolling Stones and one each by Jethro Tull, Taj Mahal and The Who. The Dirty Mac perform a tough version of 'Yer Blues' with some wailing lead guitar from Eric Clapton. They are joined by Yoko Ono and slumming violin virtuoso Ivry Gitlis for a very loose improvised boogie. Gitlis pointedly ignores Yoko's attempts to hog the microphone. Unfortunately, she succeeds and we get three minutes of atonal caterwauling.

A 2019 reissue adds previously unreleased recordings of a second take of 'Yer Blues' as well as improvised versions of the Beatles' 'Revolution' and a 'Warmup Jam'. These are ragged but much more preferable than 'Whole Lotta Yoko'.

Note that some sources credit Eric with lead guitar on an outtake of The Rolling Stones 'Parachute Woman' from the rehearsals for this show. The lead guitar on the released version is undeniably by Keith Richards, as seen in the film, and the guitar player on the outtakes is very clearly the same musician playing the same bluesy licks. Put this down as wishful thinking by an enterprising bootlegger.

Various Artists: ***Super Show 69***
Recorded 18 March 1969 at Staines Television Studios, London.

'Slate 27' (uncredited)
'Eric Rudy's Blues' (uncredited)
'Everything's Gonna Be Alright' (Jacobs)
Supershow is a very entertaining seventy-minute music documentary recorded over two days in March 1969 in a disused factory in Staines. Led Zeppelin, Buddy Guy, Stephen Stills, Jack Bruce and Buddy Miles performed on the first day; Bruce, Guy, Stills, Eric Clapton, Colosseum and Roland Kirk on the second.

'Slate 27' is a twelve-bar blues. Clapton trades exhilarating licks with Roland Kirk in an intriguing one-time jazz/blues combination. Jack Bruce, Dick Heckstall-Smith and Jon Hiseman also perform on this track. 'Eric Rudy's Blues' is a bootlegger's title for a short Clapton / Guy electric guitar jam. This marks the first time that Clapton and Guy performed together and Clapton's joy in playing with his hero is evident. Finally, a short excerpt of Little Walter's 'Everything's Gonna Be Alright' closes the film. This is listed on bootleg albums as 'End Jam' or 'The Song Of The End Of The Show'. The audio from the documentary is available on bootleg and the film itself can be watched on YouTube at the time of writing.

Billy Preston: ***That's The Way God Planned It***
George Harrison: ***All Things Must Pass***
Recorded March-April 1969 at E.M.I. Studios, Abbey Road and Olympic Sound Studios, Barnes. ***That's The Way God Planned It*** released August 1969. Did not chart. Produced by George Harrison. ***All Things Must Pass*** released November 1970. Highest position: US: 1, UK: 1. Produced by George Harrison and Phil Spector.

'Do What You Want To' (Preston)
'That's The Way God Planned It (album version)' (Preston)
'That's The Way God Planned It (single edit)' (Preston)
'I Remember Jeep' (Harrison, Baker, Clapton, Preston, Voormann)
George Harrison first met Texas-born Billy Preston in late 1962 when they were both teenagers in Hamburg. They hooked up again in January 1969 after Harrison had walked out of the fractious sessions for The Beatles' next album, preferring to see a Ray Charles concert. Preston was in Charles' band. He was invited to join The Beatles' recording sessions, where he made a significant contribution to many of the songs on the *Let It Be* album. Preston can be seen in footage of the rooftop concert that ended that band's live career on 30 January 1969, released as the finale to Peter Jackson's monumental *Get Back* documentary in 2021. Preston later played on two tracks on *Abbey Road*.

He was signed to Apple Records and in April 1969, the single 'Get Back' was credited to 'The Beatles with Billy Preston'.

That same month he recorded two songs with the incredible line-up of George Harrison, Eric Clapton, Keith Richards, Ginger Baker and Preston himself. 'Do What You Want To' is a strong opening track, a tough rock-soul with a winding guitar lick and Baker's hammering drums. The opening verses of the lead single and title track are practically a duet between Preston's gospel-tinged vocal and Eric's bluesy lead guitar. The central section includes a beautiful trade-off between Preston's swirling Hammond and Clapton's gently picked electric guitar, and the closing guitar solo has real power. Such was the strength and energy in this take that a couple of glaring mistakes were left in. 'That's the Way God Planned It', edited to three minutes, became an international hit, peaking at number 11 on the UK Singles Chart. A tentative alternative take recorded at Olympic Sound Studios in March 1969 has George Harrison, not Eric Clapton, on lead guitar. This was released in 2010 on the remastered re-release of the album.

A jam released as 'I Remember Jeep' on Harrison's *All Things Must Pass* album dates from Preston's album sessions. It was recorded on 29 March 1969 at Olympic Studios and features George and Eric with Preston, Baker and Klaus Voormann. Moog synthesizer would be overdubbed the following year during mixing sessions.

Free Creek: *Music From Free Creek*

Recorded July 1969 at The Record Plant, New York. Released January 1973. Highest position: did not chart. Produced by Earle Doud and Tom Flye.

'Road Song' (Klingman)
'Getting Back To Molly' (Klingman)
'No One Knows' (Cosgrove, Woods, Klingman)

Music From Free Creek is one of those sixties albums that remains an enigma. It was originally planned as a 'supersession' album by Todd Rundgren and comedy writer/producer Earle Dowd. Dowd recruited several big names and booked session time at the Record Plant in New York. They brought in his friend, Long Island musician Mark 'Moogy' Klingman, and when Rundgren bowed out, Klingman became musical director. Klingman, interviewed in *Heavy Metal Mayhem* magazine in 2001:

> Earl and I were friendly and he really needed me or someone like me cause he didn't know anything about music. There I was, around 19 years old at the time and I just kind of stumbled into working with all these superstars. At around 1 am, in walked Eric Clapton with an entourage. So we all went to the big room at Record Plant and everyone turned to me. I was in charge and I just made up songs on the spot. The first one we recorded was 'Road Song', a minor key blues whose lyrics I'd write the next day. I was on organ

> and Dr. John was at the piano. He blew everyone's mind with his playing. The greatest blues-funk organist/pianist I'd ever heard. I think Eric was pretty surprised and impressed with him too. Most of us didn't know that Dr. John was New Orleans' top session man. Delaney Bramlett played rhythm guitar on this song and Clapton played through a Leslie speaker for most of the songs that night and got a real down-home sound. The next song I made up on the spot. I was at the piano and said to everyone 'Here's the next tune.' And I just made up a bunch of chords that sounded good. I was making up the song as I was teaching Eric Clapton and Dr. John the song. It was a risky approach, but I took it. The song became 'No One Knows', a gospel jam that had great solos by Eric and Dr. John on the organ. Eric spoke very little but just got into playing his guitar and smiling a lot. It was late, but I told everyone I had one more song. I pulled out my harmonica and playing a one-chord blues riff I had been working on with some words I had that went, 'Getting Back to Molly'. Dr. John picked up a guitar and we had our third song. Two guitars battling with my wailing blues harp. Everyone had a great time. By the time we left the studio, it was light outside and we all had smiles on all our faces.

Vocals were added later. 'Road Song' features Tommy Cosgrove and Buzzy Linhart. Considering its ad-hoc provenance, it has a strong arrangement dominated by Dr. John's piano. Eric's solo is slow and easy, swirling and lyrical. 'No One Knows' is gospel/soul, with brilliant lead vocals by Canadian singer Eric Mercury. Clapton does his best Robbie Robertson impression. 'Getting Back To Molly' is basically a one-chord riff but really swings. Earle Dowd takes the lead vocal, with tight guitar solos by Eric Clapton and Dr. John.

The album was not released in the US In the UK it is known as both *Music From Free Creek* when first released in 1973, and *Summit Meeting* when re-issued in 1976.

Note that Roberty places this session in the first week of February 1970. Moogy Klingman says, on his website, however:

> So the call came that Eric Clapton would be coming over to Record Plant at midnight to jam. He was playing with Blind Faith at Madison Square Garden and would be coming over after the show.

Blind Faith performed at Madison Square Garden on 12 July 1969, so that's the date we've gone with here. Eric is credited as 'King Cool'.

Plastic Ono Band: *Live Peace in Toronto 1969*

Recorded 13 September 1969 at Varsity Stadium, Toronto. Released December 1969. Highest position: US: 10, UK did not chart. Produced by John Lennon and Yoko Ono.

'Blue Suede Shoes' (Perkins)
'Money (That's What I Want)' (Bradford, Gordy)
'Dizzy, Miss Lizzy' (Williams)
'Yer Blues' (Lennon, McCartney)
'Cold Turkey' (Lennon)
'Give Peace a Chance' (Lennon, McCartney)
'Don't Worry Kyoko (Mummy's Only Looking for Her Hand in the Snow)' (Ono)
'John John (Let's Hope for Peace)' (Ono)

By late 1969, John Lennon had not performed a full-length live concert for over three years since The Beatles' performance at Candlestick Park in San Francisco on 29 August 1966. Lots had happened in the intervening period: *Sgt Pepper*, Brain Epstein's death, *The White Album*, *Get Back* sessions, *Abbey Road*, Paul marrying Linda, John marrying Yoko, John deciding to leave the Beatles...

John Lennon:

> We got this phone call on a Friday night that there was a rock'n'roll revival show in Toronto with a 100,000 audience, or whatever it was, and that Chuck was going to be there and Jerry Lee and all the great rockers that were still living, and Bo Diddley, and supposedly The Doors were top of the bill. They were inviting us as king and queen to preside over it, not play – but I didn't hear that bit. I said, 'Just give me time to get a band together,' and we went the next morning.

The scratch band comprised bassist Klaus Voormann, drummer Alan White and Eric Clapton:

> One Saturday morning, the phone rang. It was John Lennon. 'What are you doing tonight?' he asked me. 'Nothing,' I replied. 'Well, do you want to do a gig with the Plastic Ono Band in Toronto?' he asked. 'Yeah, sure,' I answered, because part of the thing in those days was doing stuff like that, hopping on a plane on the spur of the moment without giving it a second thought. 'Great!' he said. 'Meet me as soon as you can get there in the BOAC first-class lounge at the London airport. I'll explain everything then.

They rehearsed in the first-class cabin on the plane and appeared on stage at midnight that same evening. The set was short and ragged but exciting. The band miss their cue to the opening 'Blue Suede Shoes', but Eric's solos are fast and smooth. Ono sits in a bag. 'Money (That's What I Want)' is slow and grungy, making up in attitude what it lacks in precision. 'Dizzy, Miss Lizzy' suffers from some patent Ono shrieking – Lennon would remove most of Yoko's vocals in the album mix, but they can be heard to their full, majestic effect on DA Pennebaker's film of the concert. Clapton's playing on

'Yer Blues' lifts the performance measurably. 'Cold Turkey' has a different arrangement to the single version that would be recorded later in the month, possibly revealing its source as 'Venus' by Shocking Blue, a hit in the Netherlands in late summer 1969 (although not a hit in the UK until early 1970). Eric is all but inaudible on 'Give Peace a Chance', although the film shows him strumming and singing strong backing vocals. Ono claps on the off beat.

Then we have 'Don't Worry Kyoko (Mummy's Only Looking for Her Hand in the Snow)' and 'John John (Let's Hope for Peace)'. We tried to pretend that these simply don't exist. Watch the film version, if you can. Clapton:

> It sounded pretty strange to me, more like howling than singing, but that was her thing.

Back at Abbey Road on 25 September, Lennon mixed the eight-track tapes from the festival performance. He recorded a first attempt at a studio version of 'Cold Turkey' later that day.

Plastic Ono Band: 'Cold Turkey' / 'Don't Worry Kyoko (Mummy's Only Looking for Her Hand in the Snow)'
John Lennon – Plastic Ono Band: *John Lennon – Plastic Ono Band Ultimate Edition*

'Cold Turkey' recorded 28 September 1969 at Trident Studios, London and 5 October 1969 at E.M.I. Studios, Abbey Road, London. 'Don't Worry Kyoko (Mummy's Only Looking for Her Hand in the Snow)' recorded 3 October 1969 at Lansdowne Studios, Lansdowne Road, London and 5 October 1969 at E.M.I. Studios, Abbey Road, London. 'Cold Turkey' / 'Don't Worry Kyoko (Mummy's Only Looking for Her Hand in the Snow)' released as a single, October 1969. Highest position: US: 30, UK: 14. ***John Lennon – Plastic Ono Band Ultimate*** Edition released 23 April 2021. Produced by John Lennon and Yoko Ono.

'Cold Turkey', 'Cold Turkey (Ultimate Mix)', 'Cold Turkey (Elements Mix)', 'Cold Turkey (Evolution Mix)', 'Cold Turkey (take 1)', 'Cold Turkey (take 2)', 'Cold Turkey (take 2) [raw mix]', 'Cold Turkey (take 2) [stripped mix]' (Lennon)
'Don't Worry Kyoko (Mummy's Only Looking for Her Hand in the Snow)' (Ono)

'Cold Turkey' is not a happy song. It was first offered to The Beatles at a band meeting on 8 September 1969, when Lennon, McCartney and Harrison were discussing a follow-up to *Abbey Road*, which had finished final mixing three weeks prior. With nothing settled, Lennon accepted a surprise invitation to perform in Toronto the following weekend, as documented on *Live Peace in Toronto 1969*. John:

> I knew before I went to Toronto, I told Allen [Klein] I was leaving [The Beatles]. I told Eric Clapton and Klaus that I was leaving and I'd like to probably use them as a group. I hadn't decided how to do it, to have a permanent new group or what. And then, later on, I thought, 'Fuck it, I'm not going to get stuck with another set of people, whoever they are.' So I announced it to myself and to the people around me on the way to Toronto the few days before.

On his return, Lennon met the rest of the Beatles at Apple's HQ on 20 September 1969. John:

> When I got back [from Toronto], there were a few meetings and Allen said, 'Cool it,' cause there was a lot to do [with The Beatles] business-wise, and it wouldn't have been suitable at the time. Then we were discussing something in the office with Paul and Paul was saying to do something, and I kept saying, 'No, no, no' to everything he said. So it came to a point that I had to say something. So I said, 'The group's over, But I couldn't help it, I couldn't stop it, it came out. And Paul and Allen said they were glad that I wasn't going to announce it, like I was going to make an event out of it. I don't know whether Paul said, 'Don't tell anybody,' but he was damn pleased that I wasn't. He said, 'Oh well, that means nothing really happened if you're not going to say anything.' So that's what happened.

Lennon pressed on with his next solo project, to record 'Cold Turkey'. An initial session at Abbey Road on 25 September did not satisfy him, so he booked a second three days later, a Sunday, at Trident Studios. For these recordings, the Plastic Ono Band consisted of Eric, Klaus and Ringo.

The subject matter of the song has been open to debate. 'Cold turkey' refers to heroin withdrawal, but Lennon's personal assistant in the late 1970s, Fred Seaman (an unreliable witness), claimed that the song was actually about a severe case of food poisoning suffered by John and Yoko after eating Christmas leftovers. This seems unlikely, as the song was recorded in September.

The final result is a tight rock and roll song, not so far from 'Yer Blues'. The final minute is harrowing, but Lennon's popularity ensured a top twenty UK hit single and an eight-week chart run. Lennon famously namechecked the song when he returned his MBE in late November 1969. In a statement, he wrote: 'I am returning the MBE in protest against Britain's involvement in the Nigeria-Biafra thing, against our support of America in Vietnam, and against 'Cold Turkey' slipping down the charts'.

Eric Clapton's response has not been documented.

Three demos and two acetates from 1969 circulate. The demos are simply two acoustic guitars: there no evidence that Eric plays here, but he might. One of these was released on *Acoustic* in 2004 and this same version, this time overdubbed with a second vocal, on the massive box set *John Lennon – Plastic*

Ono Band Ultimate Edition (where is it also slightly longer). The acetates are rough mixes of the band recordings, most likely from 29 September 1969, offering different balances with some variation in the instrumentation.

A different mix of 'Cold Turkey' can be heard on the double CD compilation *Gimme Some Truth*, released in December 2020. This is cleaner with better separation between the guitars. The musical content is identical. Takes 1 and 2, plus various different mixes of the released version, are included in the huge 6 x CD and 2 x BluRay "ultimate" box set of *John Lennon – Plastic Ono Band Ultimate Edition*, released in April 2021. Clapton's loud, funky guitar drives the two outtakes, which are not markedly different to the final release. The new mixes are interesting but hardly essential.

The b-side, Ono's 'Don't Worry Kyoko (Mummy's Only Looking for Her Hand in the Snow)' dates from 3 October 1969, using the same musicians at Lansdowne Studios in London, with further overdubs and mixing at Abbey Road two days later. It's a one-chord slide guitar jam with Ono chanting 'don't worry', wordlessly vocalising and occasionally screaming. It lasts five long minutes. This same version was released on Ono's album *Fly* in September 1971. Clapton re-joined Ono in a new line-up of the Plastic Ono Band in 2010, performing several songs at the Academy of Music in Brooklyn, with the faithful Voormann, drummer Jim Keltner and the Lennons' son Sean replacing his father. Scrappy YouTube footage confirms Clapton's skill as a slide guitarist amid the aural maelstrom of a lengthy performance of 'Don't Worry, Kyoko'.

Ric Grech: *solo project*

Recorded 7 October 1969 at Morgan Studios or perhaps 31 October 1969 at Olympic Sound Studios, London. Released in 1986 on *Blind Faith* CD. Producer unknown.

'Exchange and Mart' (credited to Grech, Clapton, Winwood, Baker)
'Spending All My Days' (credited to Grech, Clapton, Winwood, Baker)
This is a difficult one.

Rich Grech was the bassist in Blind Faith. At some point in October 1969, Grech recorded two tracks for an unfinished solo album. Different sources suggest a different date, different venues and different personnel. One documents Clapton's involvement; the other doesn't.

Clapton scholar Marc Roberty lists this session as taking place at Morgan Studios on 7 October 1969, with Clapton in attendance. Beatles scholar Simon Leng notes 31 October 1969 at Olympic Sound Studios, but does not mention Clapton. Photographer Barrie Wentzell gives us a clue, quoted at *sfea.com* (San Francisco Art Exchange):

> Robin Turner from Eric Clapton's management ran into Chris Welch and I as we were leaving a concert and said we should go to the Olympic Sound Studios in Barnes as some mystery people were jamming with Eric. We got

there and found that George Harrison, Alan White and Eric were rehearsing with Ric Grech for his solo album after Blind Faith broke up. I didn't want to disturb this hallowed ground, but Robin said it's cool and the lads don't mind, so I braved it and after saying hi to all, set up a flash umbrella and shot only a few pics as I could tell that George wasn't happy with it.

Wentzell's pictures show Clapton and Harrison, but not Grech.

Of course, all of these scenarios could be true. Or none of them. So let's include these sessions here with the rider that Eric might be playing on these tracks.

'Exchange and Mart' is a tired violin-driven blues and 'Spending All My Days' is a driving rock song that illustrates why Grech was never a lead singer. There's plenty of bluesy guitar, especially on 'Spending All My Days, ' which opens with a fluid riff and ends with a ragged solo. This is in Clapton's bluesy style, but if pushed, I'd say it's someone else's playing. Or Eric on a very bad day.

Polydor released a CD of *Blind Faith* in 1986, adding 'Exchange and Mart' and 'Spending All My Days', with writing credits to all four members of Blind Faith. Tellingly, these two songs were not included on the 2001 expanded re-release of *Blind Faith*.

Doris Troy: *Doris Troy*

Recorded October 1969, Apple Studios and Trident Studios, London. Released in September 1970. Did not chart. Produced by Doris Troy and George Harrison.

'Ain't That Cute' (Harrison, Troy)
'Give Me Back My Dynamite' (Harrison, Troy)
'I've Got To Be Strong' (Lomax, Troy)
'You Give Me Joy Joy' (Harrison, Troy, Starkey, Stills)
'Don't Call Me No More' (Troy, Schinnery)
'Get Back' (Lennon, McCartney)

Doris Troy was a gifted American singer-songwriter, a member of The Sweet Inspirations. Her only solo success was the original 'Just One Look' in 1963, later a hit for The Hollies.

She moved to London in 1969, sang on 'You Can't Always Get You Want' and signed a record deal with Apple Records. Her debut album was recorded between autumn 1969 and spring 1970, co-produced by Troy and George Harrison with contributions from Harrison, Clapton, Ringo Starr, Klaus Voormann, Bobby Keys, Jim Price, Gary Wright, Billy Preston, Stephen Stills and Peter Frampton.

'Ain't That Cute' is a powerful, commercial soul-rocker with some stinging lead guitar from Eric and tasty Harrison fills. Troy's vocal is excellent and the middle-eight is pure George. The bluesy 'Give Me Back My Dynamite' sounds like Cream with a female singer. Eric is all over this brilliant, dynamic song with loud, pulsing guitar breaks. 'I've Got To Be Strong' is a fast, fun R & B powered by the horn section and some of Eric's fat guitar riffs. 'You Give Me Joy Joy' is a soul-blue featuring four world-class guitarists. Harrison and Clapton riff along. The first solo is by Stephen Stills, the second by Peter Frampton, then with Humble Pie. Eric's contribution is negligible, but don't let this stop you from enjoying this great song. 'Don't Call Me No More' is a snappy, short, tight performance with the dream backing band of Clapton, Harrison, Preston, Voormann and Starr. Guitars are filler only here. Finally, 'Get Back' turns The Beatles' shuffle into a soul-gospel in true Otis Redding style. The solo sounds more like George's playing, but it might be Eric. This was released as a standalone single in 1969 but added to later re-releases of *Doris Troy*.

Leon Russell: ***Leon Russell***
Leon Russell: ***Leon Russell And The Shelter People***

Recorded October-November 1969, Olympic Sound Studios, Barnes. ***Leon Russell*** released in March 1970 (US), April 1970 (UK). Highest chart positions: US: 60, UK: did not chart. ***Leon Russell And The Shelter People*** released in May 1971. Highest chart positions: US: 17, UK: 29. Produced by Denny Cordell and Leon Russell.

'Prince Of Peace' (Russell, Dempsey)
'New Sweet Home Chicago' (Russell, Benno)
'Jammin' With Eric' (Russell, Clapton)
'Alcatraz' (Russell)
'Beware Of Darkness' (Harrison)

In 1969, Leon Russell was just about to break through as a solo artist following spells as an in-demand session player in Los Angeles. He had played on many popular songs of the 1960s as a member of the legendary Wrecking Crew and in the house band for the TV series *Shindig!*. Russell played on recordings by The Byrds, Gary Lewis & the Playboys, Bobby Pickett, Herb Alpert, The Ronettes and The Crystals. In 1969 he wrote 'Delta Lady' for Joe Cocker and toured as a member of Delaney And Bonnie & Friends. It was on here that he first met Eric Clapton. Russell's self-titled debut album was recorded in Los Angeles, Memphis and London between September 1969 and January 1970. Eric recorded several songs, but only one, 'Prince of Peace', was included on *Leon Russell*. Eric's playing is tight and funky – he's playing his new Stratocaster here, by the sounds of it. Think of 'Slunky' with vocals. 'New Sweet Home Chicago' and 'Jammin' With Eric', both unreleased at the time, were recorded at the same session and added to the CD re-release. 'New Sweet Home Chicago' has a New Orleans-meets-Memphis vibe, with some springy Clapton licks. 'Jammin' With Eric' is a simple but effective twelve-bar blues. Eric gets to cut loose on what could be a Bluesbreakers-period instrumental. Russell's barrelhouse piano and Jon Hiseman's jazzy drumming give a loose feel to a terrific track.

Two further songs from these sessions would be released on *Leon Russell and the Shelter People* in May 1971. Roberty places these in October-November 1969, but the CD sleeve says 23-26 August 1970 when Eric was in Miami recording the *Layla* album.

'Alcatraz' starts with some unmistakable driving lead guitar – Eric is all over this track. It's possible that other guitar parts were added during later sessions (perhaps in August 1970), or that Eric is double-tracked. 'Beware Of Darkness' is a cover of a George Harrison song recorded some months before the author's own version, although the final mix sounds like there were many subsequent overdubs following the basic take. It uses the Derek And The Dominos' rhythm section of Carl Radle and Jim Gordon. Radle and Clapton both contributed to George's version of this song the following summer. Clapton is all but inaudible here.

Duckweed Fish: *Ham Strangled Bastard*

Listed in Pete Frame's *Rock Family Trees* (1980) as one of Eric's guest sessions in this period, this is Pete's sly way of catching out people who steal his work without giving due credit.

Whilst this album and band sound intriguing, they are both fictitious.

Shawn Phillips: *Contribution*

Recorded October 1969 at Trident Studios, London. Released August 1970. Did not chart. Produced by Jonathan Weston.

'Man Hole Covered Wagon' (Phillips)

'Man Hole Covered Wagon' is breezy folk-rock by Shawn Phillips, an American singer-songwriter domiciled in the UK and friendly with Donovan, with whom he wrote and performed. Steve Winwood is credited on organ and Eric on guitar, but neither is evident on the final mix.

John Lennon and Yoko Ono: *Sometime In New York City*

Recorded 15 December 1969 at the Lyceum Ballroom, London. Released 15 September 1972 (UK), 12 June 1972 (US). Highest position: US: 48, UK: 11. Produced by John Lennon and Yoko Ono.

'Cold Turkey' (Lennon)
'Don't Worry Kyoko (Mummy's Only Looking for Her Hand in the Snow)' (Ono)

Sometime In New York City is, by some measure, John Lennon's most difficult post-Beatles album. Ten political rants and two sides of mediocre live recordings.

Side three contains versions of 'Cold Turkey' and 'Don't Worry Kyoko (Mummy's Only Looking for Her Hand in the Snow)' performed live at the Lyceum Ballroom in London on 15 December 1969. These were part of a

UNICEF charity concert, with Lennon and Ono performing with Clapton, Voormann and White from the Toronto concert, supplemented by Billy Preston, George Harrison, Keith Moon, 'Legs' Larry Smith and Tony Ashton bashing tambourines and five members of the Delaney and Bonnie and Friends band: Delaney Bramlett (guitar, vocals), Bonnie Bramlett (vocals), Bobby Keys (saxophone), Jim Gordon (drums) and Jim Price (trumpet).

The version of 'Cold Turkey' here is loud and ragged. The parping horns and rippling piano add significantly to the arrangement. The orgasmic finale goes on for four long minutes. Then we have sixteen (!) minutes of 'Don't Worry Kyoko (Mummy's Only Looking for Her Hand in the Snow)', which we've listened to so you don't have to. Ironically, this is by far the best instrumental performance of this song, although Ono's toneless shrieking negates any possible reason to actually sit through it.

Sean Head Showband: 'Labio-Dental Fricative' / 'Paper-Round'

Recorded December 1969, unknown venue. Released February 1970. Did not chart. Producer unknown.

'Labio-Dental Fricative' (Stanshall, Clapton, Cowan, Kebaka)
'Paper-Round' (Stanshall, Clapton, Cowan, Kebaka)

This time, Eric really does play on a Vivian Stanshall song, although credited as the Sean Head Showband. 'Labio-Dental Fricative' has some sweet guitar, reminiscent of the later 'Willie And The Hand Jive', with a very powerful solo from Eric. Stanshall delivers a typical stream-of-consciousness lyric. Sample: 'Cannibal chiefs chew Camembert cheese cause chewing keeps 'em cheeky'...

The b-side 'Paper-Round' is much of the same: hard rock guitar, pounding congas and a nonsense lyric. How did you find yourself this morning? Well, I just pulled back the sheets... and there I was.

The 1970s

Clapton's work rate continued through 1970, recording two albums of his own (*Eric Clapton* and *Layla And Other Assorted Love Songs*), and contributing heavily to George Harrison's All Things Must Pass, *The London Howlin' Wolf Sessions* and *Buddy Guy and Junior Wells Play The Blues*. He was off the road and out of the studio for much of 1971 and all of 1972-1973.

His return to active duty in 1974 also resulted in many more sessions as the decade progressed, perhaps most notable on Pete Townshend and Ronnie Lane's *Rough Mix*.

King Curtis: ***Get Ready***

Recorded January 1970 at Sunset Sound, Hollywood. Released March 1970. Did not chart. Produced by Delaney Bramlett.

'Teasin'' (Ousley, Bramlett)

King Curtis played memorable saxophone solos on hit singles such as 'Respect' by Aretha Franklin and 'Yakety Yak' by The Coasters. His 1970 single 'Teasin'' pairs his shrill saxophone with Clapton's biting lead guitar.

'Teasin'' can also be heard on *The History of Eric Clapton* (1972) and the 2006 deluxe edition of *Eric Clapton*. Curtis would record with Aretha Franklin and John Lennon in 1971 before being stabbed to death in an altercation outside his home that year.

Dave Mason: ***Alone Together***

Recorded in early 1970, Sunset Sound, Hollywood; Elektra Sound Recorders, Los Angeles. Released July 1970. Did not chart. Produced by Dave Mason and Tommy LiPuma.

'Only You Know And I Know' (Mason)

Dave Mason, ex-Traffic, recorded his debut solo album in Los Angeles in the early weeks of 1970 with the likes of Leon Russell, Carl Radle, Jim Gordon, Jim Keltner, Bonnie Bramlett and Rita Coolidge. The opening track and lead single 'Only You Know And I Know' was a minor hit single. The lead guitar sounds a lot like Eric's playing and he was in the same studio in the same period, recording with King Curtis and laying down tracks for his own album with many of the same musicians.

But if it is him, he has never been formally credited.

The Crickets: ***Rockin' Fifties Rock 'N' Roll***

Recorded January 1970 at Village Recorders, Los Angeles. Released December 1970. Did not chart. Produced by Delaney Bramlett.

'Rockin' 50s Rock 'N Roll' (Allison, Curtis, Gilmore)

'That'll Be The Day' (Allison, Holly, Petty)
By 1970, The Crickets comprised ex-Elvis Presley pianist Glen D. Hardin, drummer Jerry Allison and guitarist Sonny Curtis – writer of 'Walk Right Back' and 'I Fought The Law'.

Allison and Curtis were hired to sing backing vocals on Eric Clapton's first solo album, and these two songs were recorded during the same sessions with the same producer and musicians.

'Rockin' 50s Rock 'N Roll' is a generic rocker, co-written and sung by Sonny Curtis, with a fat saxophone solo and some fluid lead guitar lines from Eric.

Jerry Allison takes the lead vocal on a pointless remake of 'That'll Be The Day', which segues immediately from 'Rockin' 50s Rock 'N Roll'. Eric shuffles away in the background to limited effect.

Ashton, Gardner and Dyke: *The Worst of...*

Recorded March 1970 De Lane Lea Studios, London. Released February 1971. Highest position: did not chart. Produced by George Harrison, Tony Ashton, Kim Gardner and Roy Dyke.

'I'm Your Spiritual Breadman' (Ashton)
The credits of Ashton, Gardner and Dyke self-effacing second album 'The Worst Of...' notes guitar by 'Sir Cedric Clayton' and 'George O'Hara Smith'. These are thinly disguised pseudonyms for Eric Clapton and George Harrison.

Ashton and Dyke were members of the Liverpool band The Remo Four, sharing the same club and ballroom circuit with the pre-fame Beatles. They became friendly with George Harrison and some years later provided much of the backing for Harrison's *Wonderwall Music* (qv). Ashton and Dyke joined forces with ex-Creation bassist Kim Gardner in 1968. Ashton, Gardner and Dyke toured as the support act on Delaney and Bonnie's UK tour of November-December 1969. Three months later, they recorded 'I'm Your Spiritual Breadman' with said Sir Cedric Clayton and George O'Hara Smith. Neither is obviously audible.

Ashton, Gardner and Dyke are perhaps best remembered for 'Resurrection Shuffle', a transatlantic Top 40 success in 1971.

Jonathan Kelly: 'Don't You Believe It'

Recorded March 1970. Released June 1970. Highest position: did not chart. Produced by Colin Petersen.

'Don't You Believe It' (Kelly)
Irish folk-rock singer Jonathan Kelly moved to London in 1968 and the following year, by chance, met ex-Bee Gees drummer Colin Petersen. Kelly was performing in a restaurant and when he was seen by Petersen, who immediately offered a recording and management contract.

Kelly's second single, 'Don't You Believe It' is a driving blues-rock song with backing by Ashton, Gardner and Dyke. Eric plays some powerful slide guitar.

Kelly to Marc Roberty in *The Complete Recording Sessions 1963-1992*:

> I guess Colin Petersen asked Eric to come and play on a twelve-bar, and he just turned up, which blew my mind. He listened to the backing tracks and bang, just played it.

Petersen and Kelly would form the band Humpy Bong in 1970 with singer/bassist Tim Staffel, formerly of Smile, the band that evolved into Queen.

Ringo Starr: 'It Don't Come Easy'

Recorded 18-19 February 1970 at E.M.I. Studios, Abbey Road, London. Produced by George Martin. Unreleased.

'It Don't Come Easy' (Starkey)

Ringo laid down two versions of his big 1971 hit 'It Don't Come Easy'. The second, recorded in March 1970 and produced by George Harrison, reached number four in the UK and the US in spring 1971. Eric certainly does not play on it.

The first version, from February 1970, might have included Eric's involvement, but this is based on a report in *Melody Maker* rather than concrete proof. In any event, this early version remains unreleased and unheard.

Stephen Stills: ***Stephen Stills***

Stephen Stills: ***Stephen Stills 2***

Recorded March 1970 at Island Studios, London. ***Stephen Stills*** released November 1970. Highest position: US: 3, UK: 8. ***Stephen Stills 2*** released June 1971. Highest position: US: 8, UK: 22. Produced by Stephen Stills and Bill Halverson.

'Go Back Home' (Stills)

'Fishes and Scorpions' (Stills)

Stephen Stills took a long break from Crosby, Stills, Nash and Young in spring 1970, between the recording and release of their classic album *Déjà Vu*. He moved to London for some months and played on several sessions, including Eric's first solo album. Stills also recorded a few songs for his own self-titled debut release, holding one back for his sophomore album.

'Go Back Home' is an obvious derivative of 'Born Under A Bad Sign' with Stills' distinctive funky wah-wah guitar and gruff vocal delivery. The song builds with a turnaround after the first two verses: you have feeling building to something big when Clapton's astounding Stratocaster solo appears from nowhere and takes the song to a spell-binding conclusion.

According to Stills, who told *Louder Sound* in 2014:

> I bumped into Eric one evening, and he came by and the night degenerated into an endless jam of The Champs' 'Tequila'. Then we did the album track ['Go Back Home'] in the studio. His solo was one take and he got a fabulous sound.

Stephen Stills was a top ten album in both the UK and the US It was still in the charts when its follow-up was released. *Stephen Stills 2* includes the dynamic 'Fishes and Scorpions'. Again Eric adds somc astounding lead guitar, mixed high and very much in his 1970 style.

Billy Preston: ***Encouraging Words***

Recorded April 1970 at Apple Studios and Trident Studios, London. Released September 1970. Highest position: did not chart. Produced by George Harrison and Billy Preston.

'Right Now' (Preston)
'Use What You Got' (Preston)
'Encouraging Words' (Preston)

Billy Preston's second and last album for Apple is a stirring blend of soul and rock. It has a list of familiar participants: George Harrison, Eric Clapton, Delaney Bramlett, Carl Radle, Jim Gordon, Klaus Voormann, Ringo Starr, Bobby Keys and Jim Price. Many of these musicians would reconvene within a matter of weeks for the sessions for *All Things Must Pass*.

'Right Now' has a thick rhythm guitar that uses a riff, sound and tempo that's very close to 'Keep On Growing' from the forthcoming *Layla* album. The song closes with a short, powerful Clapton solo. 'Use What You Got' has a rolling New Orleans / Dr. John vibe. Eric's short, sweet guitar breaks employ heavy wah-wah. The joy here is infectious. 'Encouraging Words' is an effortlessly funky rock song with a positive message. Clapton deploys his sharpest blues licks, holding back until the last few moments when he really lets rip. Brilliant stuff.

Jesse Ed Davis*: ¡Jesse Davis!*

Recorded April 1970 at Olympic Sound Studios, Barnes and Village Recorders, Los Angeles. Released April 1971. Highest position: did not chart. Produced by Jesse Ed Davis.

'Reno Street Incident' (Davis)
'Tulsa County' (Pollard)
'Washita Love Child' (Davis)
'Every Night Is Saturday Night' (Davis)
'You Belladonna You' (Davis)
'Rock And Roll Gypsies' (Tillison)

'Golden Sun Goddess' (Davis)
'Crazy Love' (Morrison)

Jesse Ed Davis was a versatile session guitarist of the late 1960s and early 1970s. He was a member of Taj Mahal's band with whom he appeared as a musical guest in *The Rolling Stones Rock and Roll Circus*. Through his friendship with Leon Russell, Davis was awarded a solo recording contract with Atco. *¡Jesse Davis!* was his first solo album.

'Reno Street Incident' is a slow-burning, almost lethargic, rock song with a pleasing Leon Russell groove. Eric plays a jagged solo to close the song out. 'Tulsa County', previously recorded by The Byrds and Taj Mahal, exposes Davis' limitations as a vocalist. Eric is not immediately obvious in this. The tightly syncopated 'Washita Love Child' has a long, wailing EC solo which is mixed way back. 'Every Night Is Saturday Night' is a joyful rocker with a spiralling Dixieland horn arrangement. Eric adds a loose solo to a track that again proves that Davis was no singer. 'You Belladonna You' is the highlight of the album – pure Leon Russell with a terrific vocal hook in the chorus and powerful guitar playing from Clapton throughout, especially in the last two minutes where Eric is given free rein and plays brilliantly. The acoustic waltz-time 'Rock And Roll Gypsies' has some sweet slide guitar and suits the mood of the album. 'Golden Sun Goddess', however, is an uncharacteristic move towards Steely Dan territory, with vibes, electric sitar and 'hallelujah' backing vocals. Davis' vocals skills, unfortunately, don't match the smooth production. Clapton is inaudible unless that's him on electric sitar. In contrast, 'Crazy Love' is a straight cover of a Van Morrison song. Davis sounds eerily like Richard Manuel from The Band. Clapton plays his best Robbie Robertson fills.

Davis would never establish himself as a successful solo artist in his own right, but he would appear at George Harrison's Concert For Bangladesh (as a potential stand-in for the ailing Clapton) and later worked as a session guitar player with Jackson Browne, John Lennon, Rod Stewart, Ringo Starr and many others. He died of a suspected drug overdose in 1988.

Howlin' Wolf: ***The London Howlin' Wolf Sessions***
Muddy Waters and Howlin' Wolf: ***London Revisited***

Recorded May 1970 at Olympic Sound Studios, Barnes. ***The London Howlin' Wolf Sessions*** released August 1971. Highest position: US: 79, UK did not chart. ***London Revisited*** released February 1974. Highest position: did not chart. Produced by Norman Dayron.

'Rockin' Daddy' (Burnett)
'I Ain't Superstitious' (Dixon)
'Sittin' On Top Of The World' (Burnett)
'Worried About My Baby' (Burnett)
'What A Woman!' (Oden)

'Poor Boy' (Burnett)
'Built For Comfort' (Dixon)
'Who's Been Talking?' (Burnett)
'The Red Rooster' (Rehearsal)
'The Red Rooster' (Dixon)
'Do The Do' (Dixon)
'Highway 49' (Williams)
'Wang-Dang-Doodle' (Dixon)
'Goin' Down Slow' (Oden)
'Killing Floor' (Burnett)
'I Want To Have A Word With You' (Burnett)

The 1960s British blues boom did much to reinvigorate the careers of the post-war American blues singers. The likes of Muddy Waters, Sonny Boy Williamson, T-Bone Walker, Freddie King and Little Walter were revered by those who followed: The Rolling Stones, Steve Winwood, Eric Clapton.

A chance backstage encounter between blues guitarist Mike Bloomfield and Eric Clapton sometime in 1968 or 1969 introduced the English guitarist to Chess Records producer Norman Dayron. They discussed Howlin' Wolf and set forward a plan for Wolf to record an album with Clapton and other British musicians in London.

Months later, in May 1970, Dayron booked Olympic Studios in Barnes for several days of sessions, engineered by Glyn Johns. Clapton was joined by Ringo Starr and Klaus Voormann on the first day, and Bill Wyman and Charlie Watts on the remaining dates, with Rolling Stones pianist Ian Stewart on piano. Wolf's guitarist Hubert Sumlin plays on all tracks. Steve Winwood's contributions were overdubbed later. Keith Richards and Mick Jagger also attended at least one of the sessions but were content to watch.

The released album is superb from beginning to end. The musicians are absolutely 'on' and Howlin' Wolf's performance has equal measures of majesty and mystery.

Starr to *Louder Sound* in 2020:

> He was great. He was the Wolf Man. He was Howlin' fuckin' Wolf! We had all the baffles around the drums and I had the cans on and my eyes closed, playing to him and then suddenly it just seemed a bit... the air was hot coming across my face and I looked up and he was right over the baffles singing, right into me and the drums, so he didn't care about separation and I love that. So they're the memories. He was just, y'know, a gentle giant on those sessions.

'Rockin' Daddy' is driven by Clapton's superb lead guitar. His solo is outstanding – one of his career highlights. Willie Dixon's 'I Ain't Superstitious' sounds like Cream with a horn section. The Voormann/Starr rhythm section are as tight as you like, and Eric's solo is wonderfully fluid.

'Sittin' On Top Of The World' features the supremely talented Jeff Carp on harmonica; Eric sits back mostly but punctuates with some spitting blues licks. The up-tempo 'Worried About My Baby' is a twelve-bar shuffle. Wolf's blasting harmonica is joined by an early version of Eric's familiar solo from 'Further On Up The Road'. Eric even makes a rare mistake, but the spirit and energy of the take are what's important. A gritty version of St. Louis Jimmy Oden's 'What A Woman!' is little more than a riff. The lead playing sounds more like Hubert Sumlin's style. 'Poor Boy' is credited to Chester Burnett but is a traditional blues of unknown origin, first recorded as early as 1926. Eric plays a perfectly sharp, short solo and we should also highlight Charlie's Watts' swinging drumming. More horns are added to Willie Dixon's 'Built For Comfort' and again, the guitar solo feels more like Sumlin's work, but it might be Eric. 'Who's Been Talking?' is a close cousin of Otis Rush's 'All Your Love' with an overdubbed organ solo that sounds out of place. Eric plays filler licks. An outtake on the 2003 re-release features fascinating studio dialogue as Howlin' Wolf tutors Charlie Watts on his desired 'calypso beat'. The two minutes of dialogue that precede 'The Red Rooster' are startlingly tense.

Producer Norman Dayron to *Louder Sound* in 2020:

> On the second day in Olympic, Wolf got surly. I don't think it was about the musicians. I think it was just his mood. He was working with people that he had no real connection with. I think he was uncomfortable, and the way he expressed that was by being rather blunt and aggressive.

Glyn Johns:

> We were going to cut 'Little Red Rooster' and Eric said, 'Well, I can't play that.' Wolf looked across at him and said, 'You've more or less got it.' Eric said, 'There's no way I can do that.'

You can hear Clapton say, 'Why don't you play acoustic with us? If you play with us, we'll be able to follow you better.'

Johns:

> And so Wolf got out a beat-up old f-hole acoustic guitar and he looked out at Eric and said, 'Well, I'm going to teach you how to play it. Somebody's got to do it when I'm gone.' The whole place froze.

Clapton:

> It was a hairy experience. He came over and got hold of my wrist and said, 'You move your hand up here!' He was very, very vehement about it being done right.

The master take of 'The Red Rooster' was recorded a few days later. It's a towering performance, with Clapton's superb slide cutting, though. Clapton counts in 'Do The Do', a potent, chunky blues with a phenomenal lead vocal from Howlin' Wolf, and formidable slide guitar from Eric Clapton.

The spirit of Elmore James hovers over a lively cover of Big Joe Williams' 'Highway 49' which fades just as Eric starts to cut loose. Finally, the rolling, brooding 'Wang-Dang-Doodle' pitches Eric slide, Hubert Sumlin's subtle lead breaks and Jeff Carp's harmonica against Wolf's massive vocal delivery, which ends with some unearthly moans. Don't listen to this alone.

Clapton was out of commission when follow-ups were recorded in 1971-1973: *The London Muddy Waters Sessions*, *The London Chuck Berry Sessions* and *The London Bo Diddley Sessions*. Three of the outtakes from the Howlin' Wolf recordings, along with four by Waters, would see release on *London Revisited* in February 1974. 'Goin' Down Slow' and 'I Want To Have A Word With You' were recorded with Voormann and Starr during the first day of recording. They are less intense than the later sessions – everyone seems a touch nervous and Clapton has a tendency to overplay. The version of Wolf's signature 'Killing Floor' features Howlin' Wolf on electric guitar and vocals, backed by just Clapton, Wyman and Watts. Clapton is content to let Wolf take the spotlight, providing a tight riff but not soloing.

A deluxe double CD edition released in 2003 includes all of these, together with alternative takes and/or mixes of What A Woman', 'Who's Been Talking', 'Worried About My Baby', 'I Ain't Superstitious', 'Highway 49', 'Do The Do', 'The Red Rooster', 'Poor Boy', 'I Ain't Superstitious', 'What A Woman' and 'Rockin' Daddy'.

P. P. Arnold: *The Turning Tide*

Recorded late spring 1970 (probably), at Advision Studios, Olympic Sound Studios and I. B. C. Studios, London. Released October 2017. Did not chart. Produced by Eric Clapton.

'Medicated Goo' (Winwood, Miller)
'Brand New Day' (Morrison)
'You Can't Always Get What You Want' (Jagger, Richards)

2017's *The Turning Tide* is an album of previously unreleased recording from the late 1960s and early 1970s by P. P. Arnold, an American singer who had toured with Ike and Tina Turner and worked with The Small Faces. Her original version of Cat Stevens' 'The First Cut Is The Deepest' was a big hit in the summer of 1967.

By late 1969, Arnold was managed by Robert Stigwood, who drafted in another of his management clients to record some tracks for an album project. Eric Clapton brought Bobby Whitlock, Carl Radle, Jim Gordon, Bobby Keys and Rita Coolidge. The exact timing of these sessions is problematic. All of these musicians were together in London in December 1969 – Arnold was one of the support acts for the Delaney And Bonnie And Friends tour – and again in Los Angeles in January 1970 to record *Eric Clapton*. Most of them would go on tour with Joe Cocker in March, April and May 1970 (documented on *Mad Dogs and Englishmen*) and reconvene in London in May for sessions for George Harrison. Arnold recordings will have taken place amongst all this activity. She sings a cover of Van Morrison's 'Brand New Day'. This was released on *Moondance* in January 1970, so unless Clapton, Arnold and/or Stigwood had access to a pre-release copy, this places the sessions firmly after this date. Three London-based studios are listed on the album's sleeve notes.

'Medicated Goo' is an old school R & B version of Traffic's 1968 single. Perhaps not surprisingly, it sounds a lot like Delaney And Bonnie And Friends. Eric's playing is not evident. He is more audible on the slow-burning, gospel-tinged 'Brand New Day', playing bluesy fills and a tight solo behind the band's relaxed groove. 'You Can't Always Get What You Want' has some superb slide guitar which suggests that Eric had been listening to Duane Allman, especially his playing on Aretha's version of 'The Weight' released in January 1970.

George Harrison: *All Things Must Pass*

Recorded March 1969 at Olympic Studios, London and late May–late October 1970 at E.M.I. Studios, Trident Studios and Apple Studios, London. Released November 1970. Highest position: US: 1, UK: 1. Deluxe edition released January 2001. 50th Anniversary edition released August 2021. Produced by George Harrison and Phil Spector.

'I'd Have You Any Time' (Harrison, Dylan)
'I'd Have You Any Time' (2020 Remix) (Harrison, Dylan)
'I'd Have You Anytime' (Take 5) (Harrison, Dylan)
'My Sweet Lord' (Harrison)
'My Sweet Lord' (2001 remix) (Harrison)
'My Sweet Lord' (2020 Remix) (Harrison)
'Wah-Wah' (Harrison)
'Wah-Wah' (2020 Remix) (Harrison)
'Wah-Wah' (Take 1) (Harrison)
'What Is Life?' (Harrison)
'What Is Life?' (Take 1) (Harrison)
'What Is Life?' (2001 Remix) (Harrison)
'What Is Life?' (2020 Remix) (Harrison)
'Let It Down' (Harrison)
'Let It Down' (2020 Remix) (Harrison)
'Run Of The Mill' (Harrison)
'Run Of The Mill' (2020 remix) (Harrison)
'Run Of The Mill' (Take 36) (Harrison)

'Beware Of Darkness' (Harrison)
'Beware Of Darkness' (2020 remix) (Harrison)
'Beware Of Darkness' (Take 8) (Harrison)
'All Things Must Pass' (Harrison)
'All Things Must Pass' (2020 remix) (Harrison)
'I Dig Love' (Harrison)
'I Dig Love' (2020 remix) (Harrison)
'Art Of Dying' (Harrison)
'Art Of Dying' (2020 remix) (Harrison)
'Awaiting On You All' (Harrison)
'Awaiting On You All' (2020 remix) (Harrison)
'Isn't It A Pity (Version Two)' (Harrison)
'Isn't It A Pity (Version Two)' (2020 remix) (Harrison)
'Isn't It A Pity (Version Two)' (Take 14) (Harrison)
'Isn't It A Pity (Version Two)' (Take 27) (Harrison)
'Hear Me Lord' (Harrison)
'Hear Me Lord' (2020 mix) (Harrison)
'Hear Me Lord' (take 5) (Harrison)
'Plug Me In' (Harrison, Clapton, Gordon, Mason, Radle, Whitlock)
'Thanks For The Pepperoni' (Harrison, Clapton, Gordon, Mason, Radle, Whitlock)
'Out Of The Blue' (Harrison, Aronowitz, Clapton, Gordon, Keys, Price, Radle, Whitlock, Wright)
'Get Back' (Lennon, McCartney)
'Down To The River (Rocking Chair Jam)' (Harrison)

By mid–1970, with The Beatles well and truly over, George Harrison had a huge stockpile of songs ready to go. Some of these, such as 'All Things Must Pass', 'Hear Me Lord', 'Isn't It a Pity' and 'Let It Down', were offered to The Beatles during rehearsals in January 1969. 'Wah-Wah' was written immediately after quitting those fraught sessions on 10 January 1969. George told Howard Smith at WABC-FM radio in New York City on 1 May 1970:

> I've had songs for a long time, and lots of new songs. I've got about... enough songs for about three or four albums, actually. But if I do one, that'll be good enough for me.

George entered Abbey Road in late May 1970. Sessions took place, more or less, in three batches, with Eric Clapton in attendance for the first and third sets. The first sessions ran from 28 May 1970 through to early June. Harrison and Clapton were joined by Bobby Whitlock, Billy Preston, Gary Brooker, Ringo Starr, Klaus Voormann and Alan White. The members of Badfinger also contributed to initial sessions, layering acoustic guitars, and horn players Bobby Keys and Jim Price were present as necessary.

The first track recorded was the raucous 'Wah-Wah', Phil Spector's wall-of-sound is much in evidence. 'Wah-Wah' is a glorious, driving, majestic rocker that George wrote after temporarily quitting The Beatles. It has a dense, reverb-flooded production with Eric Clapton on electric guitar (it sounds like George plays the opening riff with Eric joining with wah pedal after five seconds). Badfinger's Joey Molland recalled, 'It was an enormous amount of sound in your headphones. It was super powerful. It was great.' The released master is take three. An alternative take one was released on the 50th-anniversary reissue.

The lead single 'My Sweet Lord' still sounds truly astonishing. It was the second song of the sessions, recorded on the same day as 'Wah-Wah' with sixteen complete takes. George's hymn to Krishna opens with layers of chiming acoustic guitar and we get to hear George's signature slide guitar for the first time as the sound builds with strings and backing vocals. According to Alan White and Klaus Voormann, one of the rhythm guitars is played by John Lennon. Eric played the song's signature slide part during run-throughs, but the final slide guitar parts heard on the finished recording were tracked as overdubs later in the year at Trident Studios. Unless Clapton added an acoustic guitar part, then it's likely that his contributions were not used.

'My Sweet Lord' was a number one single in the US and the UK and was 1971's best-selling song. The original 1970 track was spruced up with some parts re-recorded, notably the slide guitar and new vocals from Sam Brown, for the 30th-anniversary edition of *All Things Must Pass*. The 2002 re-release of the original track reached no. one in the UK, for one week, the most recent Beatles-related number one single.

The third song attempted at the first session was the album's opening track, the delicate 'I'd Have You Anytime' co-written by Harrison with Bob Dylan. Clapton plays the bluesy opening guitar licks and adds distinctive accents. The released master is take seven; take five was released on the 50th-anniversary reissue in 2021.

The first version of 'Isn't It A Pity', on which Eric does not appear, dates from 2 June. Later that day, after Clapton had arrived, they recorded the libidinous and sassy 'I Dig Love'. George plays acoustic guitar, Eric is on slinky electric guitar and Harrison's slide guitar solo was added during later overdubs.

The following day this same group of musicians recorded the powerful and deeply moving 'Isn't It a Pity (version two)': anyone who has lived through regret can respond to its universal message of love and forgiveness. The lyrics, poetic and heartfelt, talk of spiritual salvation and friendship. This second version is slow, sedate and stately. Eric's lyrical guitar fills – routed through a Leslie speaker – duet deliciously with George's heartfelt vocals. The released master is take 30 and an alternative take 27 is included on the 50th-anniversary reissue. Clapton performed this song, brilliantly, as part of his live set in the late 2000s.

Clapton would not be present for sessions with steel guitarist Pete Drake in early-mid June. The songs 'If Not For You', 'Behind That Locked Door', 'Ballad of Sir Frankie Crisp (Let It Roll)', 'I Live For You' and 'All Things Must Pass' date from these sessions. Clapton would, however, add backing vocals to 'All Things Must Pass' at a later date.

Clapton himself, meanwhile, had a solo album due for release and promote. He reunited with members of Delaney and Bonnie Bramlett's band with whom he (and George) had toured the previous December. Rehearsing at Clapton's home, Hurtwood Edge, this new band, as yet unnamed, debuted at The Lyceum in London on 14 June.

These musicians, soon to become Derek and the Dominos, would form the core band for the remainder of the *All Things Must Pass* sessions running from the third week in June through to the start of July.

'What Is Life', recorded 22 June, is a bright, exultantly commercial song written as George was on his way to a Billy Preston recording session in 1969. George plays the signature lick and Clapton adds rapid rhythm guitar. An alternative mix of 'What Is Life' was included on the 2001 reissue of *All Things Must Pass*. This removes the vocals and adds trumpet and oboe. An alternative take one can be heard on the 50th-anniversary reissue.

The gospel-influenced spiritual rock song 'Awaiting on You All' is almost buried under Phil Spector's massive production. Eric plays an enormous slide guitar, with the harmony part added later. Clapton probably plays the clean, bright slide during the introduction of the colossal production of 'Let It Down'. An alternative take one is included on the 50th-anniversary reissue. This does not include the opening slide guitar, so it's assumed that Clapton does not participate, but he might.

Is 'Run of the Mill' about Paul? Patti? 'Everyone has choice when to or not to raise their voices / It's you that decides which way you will turn / While feeling that our love's not your concern / It's you that decides.' The production is mostly acoustic, with added horns – a welcome contrast to the walls of overdubs heard elsewhere on this album. Eric presumably plays acoustic here.

'Beware of Darkness' is a beautiful ballad, with George joined by Eric's restrained lead guitar. Clapton sang this song with genuine love and emotion at George's memorial concert in 2002. 'Art of Dying' opens with a blistering wah-wah lead guitar part from Clapton. Jim Gordon and Carl Radle drive the powerful rhythm, accompanied by Bobby Whitlock's swirling Hammond organ. The 2020 remix showcases some strong playing by everyone, but by Clapton in particular. This is also the case with the astonishing and unambiguous 'Hear Me Lord', one of those lost classics of the period. George plays slide against Eric's distorted rhythm. The near-ten minute take five is on the 50th-anniversary release alongside a fun, loose jam of 'Get Back', recorded 1 July 1970. Eric cannot be obviously picked out on this latter track.

Delighting in each other's playing, George, Eric and the nascent Dominos recorded several jams with Dave Mason, Klaus Voormann, Bobby Keys, Jim

Price and Gary Wright. Sides five and six of the original triple album includes three of these along with 'I Remember Jeep' most likely recorded the previous March during sessions for Billy Preston's *That's The Way God Planned It*: they are lengthy and unremarkable. Klaus Voormann claims that he plays lead guitar on 'Out Of The Blue', not Clapton. 'I'm actually playing the guitar on that one,' Voormann says. 'When George was trying to remember who played on it, when he was doing the credits, he heard this fast lick I was doing and thought, 'Ah, that must be Eric. But that was me.''

Finally, 'Down To The River' is a very loose blues jam included on the 50th-anniversary re-release. If you've never heard it, then you've not missed anything. Eric is presumably playing dobro here.

With basic tracks for the album concluded, overdubbing started at the end of July at Trident and Apple. The album was mixed in October and released to great acclaim and huge success the following month. The 50th-anniversary remixes the entire album (except the jams), stripping away the bombastic reverb and many of the overdubs, letting the songs breathe.

George Harrison's talent as a musician and songwriter, hidden in plain sight for years, is evident in this extravagant, highly personal and very successful album. In 1971, the chief ex–Beatle wasn't Lennon or McCartney, but George Harrison, 12 Arnold Grove, Wavertree, Liverpool 15.

Dr. John: *The Sun, Moon & Herbs*

Recorded July 1970 at Trident Studios, London. Released August 1971. Did not chart. Produced by Mac Rebennack (Dr. John) and Charles Greene.

'Black John The Conqueror' (Rebennack)
'Where Ya At Mule' (Rebennack)
'Craney Crow' (Rebennack)
'Familiar Reality (opening)' (Rebennack, Hill)
'Pots on Fiyo / Who I Got To Fall On' (Rebennack)
'Zu Zu Manou' (Rebennack)
'Familiar Reality (reprise)' (Rebennack, Hill)

Dr. John's music irresistibly combined blues, pop, jazz, boogie-woogie, funk and rock and roll. Born Mac Rebennack in 1941, before coming to prominence, he had spent time in jail for selling drugs and running a brothel. He redefined himself as Dr. John the Night Tripper in 1968, playing a unique psychedelic variant on New Orleans R & B. His album *Gris-Gris* sets the template for his future career. *The Sun, Moon & Herbs* is his fourth album. Clapton is credited as guitarist on all tracks but is only audible on a few.

'Where Ya At Mule' has some lovely Dobro, mixed low but unmistakably EC. The slow, moody 'Craney Crow' has some delicate Claptonesque slide phrases. Eric briefly lets loose on the short 'Familiar Reality (reprise)'.

The slide guitar on 'Familiar Reality (opening)' is definitely not in Eric's style, but it might be him.

'Black John The Conqueror' and 'Pots on Fiyo / Who I Got To Fall On' are a swampy tracks, but Eric's involvement is not obvious. Likewise, the spooky 'Zu Zu Manou' has some jazzy guitar chords, but this is unlikely to be Clapton's playing.

Buddy Guy and Junior Wells: ***Play The Blues***

Recorded October 1970 at Criteria Studios, Miami. Released August 1972. Highest position: did not chart. Deluxe reissue released 2014. Produced by Eric Clapton, Ahmet Ertegun and Tom Dowd.

'A Man Of Many Words' (Guy)
'My Baby She Left Me' (Williamson)
'Come On In This House / Have Mercy Baby' (Wells)
'T-Bone Shuffle' (Walker)
'A Poor Man's Plea' (Wells)
'Messin' With The Kid' (London)
'I Don't Know' (Mabon)
'Bad Bad Whiskey' (Davis)

Bonus tracks on the 2014 reissue:
'Dirty Mother For You' (Wilborn)
'Stone Crazy' (Guy)
'Why Am I Treated So Bad (Playing The Blues)' (Staples)
'Tears, Tears, Tears' (Milburn)
'Love Her With Feeling' (Whittaker)
'Checking Up On My Baby' (Williamson)
'Last Night' (Jacobs)
'First Time I Met The Blues' (Montgomery)
'D Blues' (Guy)
'Bad Bad Whiskey (long version)' (Davis)
'You're So Fine' (Jacobs)
'Sweet Home Chicago' (Johnson)

If Robert Johnson and J. J. Cale are the two most important influences on Eric Clapton's career, then Buddy Guy must surely be a close third. In 1965, Guy had been playing in London with a trio line-up. Eric was impressed, as he recalled:

> I had first seen Buddy Guy playing at the Marquee. Even though he was accompanied by only a bass player and a drummer, he created a huge,

> powerful sound, and it blew me away. It was almost as if he didn't need anyone else. He could have played the whole set on his own. He made it look so easy, and as I was watching, I was thinking, 'I can do that,' and now that my confidence was high, I began to really believe that I could make that leap, and I was truly inspired.

Clapton formed Cream soon afterwards.

By 1970, Guy was in partnership with harmonica player Junior Wells. Hot off a European tour supporting The Rolling Stones, they entered Criteria Studios in Miami that October to record an album. *Play The Blues* captures two important blues musicians at their best. Clapton co-produces and mostly sticks to Dobro, or unobtrusive rhythm guitar (or, potentially, doesn't play at all). Certainly, all of the electric guitar solos on the original album are by Buddy Guy.

'A Man Of Many Words' is a funk/blues rewrite of Otis Redding's 'Hard To Handle'. The lead guitar sounds, to me, like Buddy Guy. Bass and drums are by Carl Radle and Jim Gordon of Derek and the Dominos. Sonny Boy Williamson's sprightly 'My Baby She Left Me' showcases Junior Wells, with the guitarists in the pocket. Wells is to the fore again in the mid-tempo medley 'Come On In This House / Have Mercy Baby'. Clapton again sticks to rhythm, low in the mix. Guy stretches out on his rendition of T-Bone Walker's signature workout, 'T-Bone Shuffle'. Eric is not audible here. Junior Wells' 'A Poor Man's Plea' is a one-note shuffle. Eric is, again, either low in the mix or simply not playing. The same applies when Wells revisits his classic 'Messin' With The Kid', which features Dr. John on piano and to a down-home version of Willie Mabon's 'I Don't Know'. 'Bad Bad Whiskey' has Clapton on unmistakable Dobro. Guy delivers electrifying lead guitar. A longer version of this is included on the 2014 reissue – it's the same take fading a couple of minutes later.

The reissue includes several bonus tracks, all credited to the October 1970 sessions. Most of these are excellent: it's not clear why these were not released at the time. There are certainly two guitarists on 'Dirty Mother For You' – the first guitar solo is pure Clapton, the second is Buddy Guy. 'Stone Crazy' burns for ten minutes. There is only one guitar player and Guy gets the nod here. This is a very good song indeed. The funky take of The Staple Singers' 'Why Am I Treated So Bad (Playing The Blues)' is presented in two mixes, one brighter and shorter, the other running to seven minutes with extra verses. Eric sticks to tight electric rhythm guitar. Amos Milburn's 'Tears, Tears, Tears' has a false start and cops the riff from 'Smokestack Lightning'. Again, it sounds like Eric on rhythm and Guy on lead. The nine-minute version of Tampa Red's 'Love Her with a Feeling' has two guitarists, but only Guy takes a solo. Likewise, a tough, funky cover of Sonny Boy Williamson's 'Checking Up On My Baby' has a tight, syncopated arrangement but probably no Eric. 'Last Night' is a slow, tense Little Walter song with Eric on Dobro, including a solo, and Guy on electric guitar and half-remembered lyrics. 'The First Time I Met The Blues' was written by Little Brother Montgomery and was first released in 1937. It sounds like three guitarists here, but only Guy and Clapton are credited and neither the solo nor the muted call-and-response are Eric's playing to these ears. In contrast, the nine-minute 'D Blues' has some lead breaks that sit right in Clapton's style (Guy says 'take it baby' before a fine extemporised solo). It's surely Eric. He is less obvious on Little Walter's short and sharp 'You're So Fine' and might not be playing at all. Finally, 'Sweet Home Chicago', even then, something of a tired war horse, seems to have two guitar players, but the arrangement is busy and neither takes a solo, so a definitive conclusion on just who's playing is difficult to agree.

Eric Dennis of *Spectrum Culture* said in July 2012:

> Much like *Kind of Blue* is for jazz newcomers, in many ways, *Play the Blues* is the perfect starter album for anyone unfamiliar with blues music or for those looking for only a quick fix. It might not be worshipped to the same degree of that Miles Davis masterpiece, but it's a charming, and sometimes deeply moving, album that's easy to get hooked on.

Another two songs, 'This Old Fool' and 'Honeydripper', were recorded with the J. Geils Band at Intermedia Studios, Boston, in April 1972. Eric does not contribute.

James Luther Dickinson: *Dixie Fried*

Recorded October 1970 at Criteria Studios, Miami. Released February 1972. Highest position: did not chart. Produced by Tom Down and Jim Dickinson.

'The Judgement' (Dickinson, Utley)

Jim Dickinson was a member of the Dixie Flyers, the house band at Criteria Studios in Miami – the recording venue for *Layla And Other Assorted Love Songs* in August and September 1970. 'The Judgement' was recorded during sessions for Buddy Guy's and Junior Wells' *Play The Blues*, with some of the same musicians and producer. It has a slow, bluesy Dr. John vibe (Mac is on piano here) with decidedly uncertain vocals. The guitar solo is not in Eric's usual fluid style.

The Rolling Stones: *Sticky Fingers* sessions

Recorded December 1970 at Olympic Sound Studios, Barnes. Released June 2015. Highest position: US: 5, UK:7. Produced by Jimmy Miller.

'Brown Sugar' (Jagger, Richards)

'Brown Sugar' is a rock classic , the opening track and lead single from the brilliant album *Sticky Fingers*, released in April 1971. Sessions for *Sticky Fingers* lasted from March 1969 to October 1970, and the album was finished when this alternative version of 'Brown Sugar' was recorded at Olympic Studios on Keith Richards' twenty-eighth birthday.

It's certainly a surprise hearing Eric's powerful slide guitar during the familiar opening riffs of this seemingly spontaneous performance. The more polished version from the previous December would be used as the single and this take stayed in the vaults until 2015.

Bobby Whitlock: ***Bobby Whitlock***
Bobby Whitlock: ***Raw Velvet***

Recorded January 1971 at Olympic Sound Studios, Barnes. ***Bobby*** Whitlock released February 1972. Highest position: did not chart. ***Raw Velvet*** released November 1972. Highest position: did not chart. Produced by Andy Johns and Bobby Whitlock.

'Where There's A Will There's A Way' (Whitlock)
'A Day Without Jesus' (Whitlock, Nix)
'Back In My Life Again' (Whitlock)
'The Scenery Has Slowly Changed' (Whitlock)
'The Dreams Of A Hobo' (Whitlock)
'Hello LA, Bye Bye Birmingham' (Bramlett, Davis)

Bobby Whitlock was a key player in Derek and the Dominos ('the most energetic sideman I have ever seen', as Clapton once admitted), writing or co-writing half of the songs on *Layla And Other Assorted Love Songs* and both sides of their withdrawn single 'Tell The Truth' backed with 'Roll It Over'. Whitlock's powerful, soulful vocals and keyboard playing were integral components of that short-lived band.

So it was only natural that Eric Clapton and the rest of the Dominos should perform on Whitlock's first solo album recorded at Olympic in the first weeks of 1971. George Harrison also contributes. As Whitlock would write:

> The Dominos' second album sessions were booked for April and May, so I thought it was a good time to start recording my first solo album. My idea was to get all the people I had played with on it. The first person that I called was Eric and asked him if he would play on my album and he said yes straight away. The next person I was to call was George [Harrison] and he said that he would love to come and play on my record. I called Carl [Radle] next, and he said that he would be there as soon as he was finished. For the most part, the album was recorded with just Jim [Gordon] and Klaus [Voormann] and me, except for the live recordings with George and Eric on them. Then it was the full band with no overdubs.

'Where There's A Will There's A Way' has a long history. It was part of the Delaney and Bonnie tour in November and December 1969 and was released on the album *On Tour With Eric Clapton* the following April (credited there to Bramlett / Bramlett/ Whitlock, with another three versions from this tour released in

2010). The first studio version dates from November 1969, with most of the same musicians recording at Olympic during sessions for Clapton's first solo album. There are no lead vocals. Whitlock's solo version at the same studio over a year later rolls and rocks with abandon. Eric Clapton's slide guitar is unmistakeable.

Whitlock:

> This was recorded in the small room, or Studio B at Olympic Studios. Eric is playing slide guitar and is sitting about six feet from me in front of and to my right with his back to the drum booth. George is playing rhythm guitar and is standing three feet directly in front of me and is looking me in the eyes the whole time. Klaus Voormann is on bass and Jim Gordon is in the drum booth, where he stayed the whole time. The horns were overdubbed.

Two other songs were recorded the same day. 'A Day Without Jesus' is a breathless gospel with Eric sitting in the mix. 'Back In My Life Again', which has some taut guitar lines in the fade-out, was written on the spot as Whitlock recalls:

> George had turned to me after we did 'A Day Without Jesus' and said, 'What's next?' I hadn't planned on doing another number and didn't have one in my head, so I told him that I didn't know what was next. I drew a blank. Here I had Eric Clapton and George Harrison in my first session and I'm drawing a complete blank! I guess that's the best thing that could have happened because I had opened myself up for that creative influence to come into play. George said, 'Why don't you just make something up?' I was sitting at the organ and said, 'OK, B minor.' I gave Jim a tempo and he counted it off and we all started playing and it fell together as if it had already been written. Andy had a mike set up for me to sing through and the words came out at the same time as we were recording it. The story and the melody and all just fell out together at the same time. It was truly an amazing moment.

Whitlock recalls writing 'The Scenery Has Slowly Changed' at Clapton's house Hurtwood Edge, shortly after the Delaney and Bonnie tour. It starts gently with some brilliant lead guitar. It then pumps up to a dynamic conclusion; Eric's playing is terrific.

> This is the most beautiful guitar work that I have ever heard Eric play. What he played was for me, I'm sure, because he was playing how I felt.

Marc Roberty credits Clapton with guitar on 'The Dreams Of A Hobo' from this album. There is some gorgeous Dobro and it might be Eric, but it doesn't really fit his style.

A sixth song, 'Hello LA, Bye Bye Birmingham', date from these sessions but would he held over for Whitlock's second album *Raw Velvet*. It includes Eric's only know credit on bass guitar. With Eric's raw slide guitar, this sounds like an outtake from *Layla And Other Assorted Love Songs*.

John Mayall: *Back To The Roots*
John Mayall: *Archive To Eighties*

Recorded January 1971, INC Studios, London. *Back To The Roots* released March 1971. Highest position: US: did not chart, UK: 31. ***Archive To Eighties*** released January 1988. Produced by John Mayall.

'Prisons On The Road' (Mayall)
'Accidental Suicide' (Mayall)
'Home Again' (Mayall)
'Looking At Tomorrow' (Mayall)
'Force of Nature' (Mayall)
'Goodbye December' (Mayall)

Note that some sources date these sessions to mid-November 1970. I have used Roberty's dates here.

'Prisons On The Road' is a straightforward blues shuffle, with Mayall's usual uncertain vocals. There is a violin solo. Eric spits out some furious trebly guitar licks. 'Accidental Suicide' is an embarrassing tribute to Jim Hendrix ('watch what you do, you may be the next to go'). Clapton does his best to inject some life into a standard fast twelve-bar blues, which lasts six long minutes and includes a violin solo. 'Home Again' sticks to piano, adding walking bass, a lengthy, stinging guitar solo and a horrible lead vocal. In contrast, 'Looking At Tomorrow' moves away from I-IV-V and has a feeling of Mayall's work on *Blues From Laurel Canyon*, with some powerful and very effective double-tracked Clapton guitar work. And a violin solo. Clapton and Mayall are joined by both Mick Taylor on slide guitar and Mayall's then-current guitarist Harvey Mandell for 'Force of Nature'. The three guitarists try not to trip each other up. 'Goodbye December' is a mellow track with Mayall on guitar and Eric's gentle wah-wah accompaniment.

Fourteen years later, Mayall re-recorded parts of five of these tracks for his 1988 album *Archive To Eighties*: 'Prisons On The Road', 'Accidental Suicide', 'Home Again', 'Looking At Tomorrow' and 'Force of Nature'. Mayall recorded new bass and drums for no discernible reason, as well as replacing his vocal, harmonica and keyboard tracks. The songs are also remixed and sound much brighter: Eric is much more prominent but the drums, now with the loud snap of eighties reverb, sound like they belong to a different set of songs. 'Looking At Tomorrow' in particular loses much of its character.

George Harrison and Friends: *The Concert For Bangladesh*

Recorded 1 August 1971, Madison Square Garden, New York. Released December 1971 (US), January 1972 (UK). Highest position: US: 2, UK: 1. Produced by George Harrison and Phil Spector.

'Wah-Wah' (Harrison)
'My Sweet Lord' (Harrison)
'Awaiting on You All' (Harrison)
'That's the Way God Planned It' (Preston)
'It Don't Come Easy' (Starkey)
'Beware of Darkness' (Harrison)
'While My Guitar Gently Weeps' (Harrison)
'Medley: Jumpin' Jack Flash/Youngblood' (Jagger, Richards, Leiber, Stoller)
'Something' (Harrison)
'Bangla Desh' (Harrison)

Organized by George Harrison and Ravi Shankar, the Concert For Bangladesh was the first big-name rock benefit show. It was held in aid of the refugees of Bangladesh following a destructive cyclone and the then-active Bangladesh Liberation War. All proceeds went to UNICEF.

This was George Harrison's first publicly announced live performance for five years. Riding high on the success of *All Things Must Pass* – seven weeks at number one in the US in January and February 1971, seven weeks at number one in the UK in February and March 1971 – Harrison pulled together a band of famous friends to perform at Madison Square Garden for two shows on Sunday 1 August 1971: Eric Clapton on guitar, Ringo Starr and Jim Keltner on drums, Leon Russell and Billy Preston on keyboards, Klaus Voormann on bass, Badfinger (Pete Ham, Tom Evans, Joey Molland and Mike Gibbins) on acoustic guitars and percussion, the Hollywood Horns and 'The Soul Choir'. Harrison performed seven of his own songs, and Ringo Starr, Leon Russell and Billy Preston took their places in the spotlight, too. Harrison also persuaded Bob Dylan to return to the stage for one of only a handful of public performances between May 1966 and January 1974. Ravi Shankar played a well-received set of Indian classical music.

Eric Clapton, however, was in the midst of self-imposed heroin-induced exile following the death of Jim Hendrix, the break-up of Derek And The Dominos and an infatuation with George Harrison's wife, Patti. As he writes in his memoirs:

> George called me one day to ask if I'd fly to New York to play in a show he was putting on to raise money for the victims of the Bangladesh famine. He was only too aware of my drug problems and may have seen this as some kind of rescue mission. Whatever the reason, I told him I could go only if he could guarantee that they could keep me supplied. Since the initial schedule was about a week's rehearsal followed by the show, he was pretty certain he could take care of it. By the time we got to the hotel in New York… there was a good supply waiting in my room. I tried some, but nothing happened. It turned out that what they had scored for me was street-cut, with a very low amount

of actual heroin in it and cut with something nasty, like strychnine, so that it was about a tenth as strong as what I was used to. The result was that I went cold turkey for the first two or three days and missed all the rehearsals. Allen Klein… offered me some medication he was taking for his ulcers. I took some and, amazingly, at the eleventh hour, it made me feel okay.

Clapton did not appear until a rehearsal/soundcheck the night before the shows. Jesse Ed Davis had been drafted as a sub in case Clapton couldn't perform (or didn't show). Eric played a semi-hollow body Gibson Byrdland during the afternoon concert, switching to his tobacco sunburst Fender Stratocaster, Brownie, for the evening show. Perhaps not surprisingly, he does not sing at all, although his own 'Let It Rain' was on the proposed setlist. Nor does he particularly shine on guitar on any of ten songs on which he plays: using the Byrdland on 'While My Guitar Gently Weeps' gave a thin, trebly sound. Nevertheless, the interplay between Eric and George is magnificent.

Eric:

I have a vague memory of… playing the show. No matter how I've tried to rationalize it to myself over the years, I let a lot of people down that night, most of all myself. I've seen the concert only once on film, but if I ever want a reminder of what I might be missing from the 'good old days', this would be the film to watch.

Other than an unreleased and unheard session with Stevie Wonder in October 1972 and pair of shows at the Rainbow in London three months later, the Concert For Bangladesh was Clapton's last professional or public appearance for two and a half years.

The *Concert For Bangladesh* album, meanwhile, was number one in the UK and the US, and won the Grammy for Album of the Year at the 1973 awards.

The Who: *Tommy Original Soundtrack Recording*

Recorded March 1974 at Ramport Studios, Battersea. Released March 1975. Highest position: US: 2, UK: 21. Produced by The Who.

'Eyesight To The Blind' (Williamson)
'Eyesight To The Blind [film version]' (Williamson)
'Sally Simpson' (Townshend)

Pete Townshend's first great song-cycle project, *Tommy*, has taken on a life of its own. First released as a double album in 1969, it was toured by The Who in opera houses and at festivals across Europe and the US. An orchestral version with guest singers was released in 1972.

Ken Russell's 1975 film version of *Tommy* is outrageously over-the-top. Who can forget Elton John blasting out 'Pinball Wizard' on massive bovver boots or Ann-Margret cavorting in baked beans?

The soundtrack comprises the entire original album re-recorded by Pete Townshend at The Who's own Ramport Studios in London between January and March 1974. Even though the album is credited to The Who, there are some tracks where they don't play as a collective.

Clapton sings and plays on 'Eyesight To The Blind', as well as appearing in the film as The Preacher, the leader of a Marilyn Monroe-themed cult. Yes, really.

The version used in the film extends the song by two minutes to 5.30 and features Arthur Brown on additional vocals and lots more guitar soloing from Eric.

Pete Townshend recalled in his autobiography:

> Eric's manager pressed him into taking a role in *Tommy*. Eric wasn't keen but did it partly for me since I'd helped him put up the Rainbow concert. The song he would play was 'Eyesight to the Blind', and Eric wanted to create a new riff for the song to make it his own; he had the notion that he would like his guitar doubled by clavinet, the electric keyboard used famously by Stevie Wonder. As it happened, Stevie was in town, so Eric took me with him to Island Studios to try to persuade Stevie to work on the track. When we got to the studio ... Stevie ignored me. He was sweet to Eric, but even so, he refused to contribute in any way. In the event, I tried to emulate his inimitable wah-wah clavinet style on the track, which certainly wasn't easy.

The musicians on 'Sally Simpson' are Eric (unmistakably him on Blackie), the brilliant Nicky Hopkins on piano and the rhythm section of Graham Deacon – who played on John Entwistle's early solo albums – and Phil Chen, who was in Jeff Beck's band at that time. Townshend and Daltrey are on vocals.

Freddie King: ***Burglar***
Freddie King: ***1934-1976***
Eric Clapton: ***Give Me Strength-The '74-'75 Recordings***

Recorded August 1974 at Criteria Studios, Miami. Burglar released 1974. Highest position: did not chart. ***Freddie King (1934-1976)*** released October 1977. Highest position: did not chart. ***Give Me Strength-The '74-'75 Recordings*** released 2013. Highest position: did not chart. Produced by Tom Dowd.

'Sugar Sweet' (London)
'TV Mama' (Turner)
'I Wonder Why' aka 'Gambling Woman Blues' (Josea, King) – edited
'I Wonder Why' aka 'Gambling Woman Blues' (Josea, King) – full length
'Boogie Funk' (King)

Texan blues musician Freddie King was a major influence on Eric Clapton's playing style – King's 1961 instrumental 'Hideaway' was repurposed as Eric

Clapton's spotlight on the *Bluesbreakers with Eric Clapton* album. The biting Les Paul tones of that recording were the flames under Eric's early career. As Eric noted in his memoirs:

> The most significant event for me was when [bandmate] Tom [McGuinness] one day brought out a record by black artist Freddie King, a 45 rpm instrumental called 'Hideaway' that he was mad about. I'd never heard Freddy King before, and listening to him had an effect on me similar to what I might feel if I were to meet an alien from outer space. It simply blew my mind. I [tried] to emulate the sharp, thin sound that Freddie King got out of his Gibson Les Paul, and I ended up with something quite different.

Eight years later, Clapton and King recorded several songs together during sessions at Criteria in August 1974. One of these, a cover of Mel London's 'Sugar Sweet' was released on King's *Burglar* album later that year. Clapton plays funky rhythm guitar here, the solos are by King, and George Terry adds slide guitar.

'Sugar Sweet' was re-released in 1977 on the posthumous compilation *1934-1976*, with two other songs from the 1974 sessions. 'TV Mama' is a powerful, up-tempo blues song first released by Joe Turner and His Blues Kings in 1953. Clapton plays a trademark solo in the middle of the song. A slow-burning cover of B. B. King's 'I Wonder Why' (miscredited here as 'Gambling Woman Blues') is an eight-minute edit of a much longer track. Freddie King and Eric Clapton complement each other perfectly. George Terry adds some slippery slide guitar. A full-length, unedited version remixed to bring Clapton's guitar more prominence was released in 2013 on *Give Me Strength-The '74-'75 Recordings*, alongside 'Sugar Sweet', 'TV Mama' and a previously unreleased fast blues jam 'Boogie Funk'. Again, it is listed here as 'Gambling Woman Blues'.

George Harrison: *Dark Horse*

Recorded October 1974 at A&M Studios, Los Angeles. Released December 1974. Highest position: US: 4, UK: did not chart. Produced by George Harrison.

'Bye Bye Love' (Bryant, Bryant, Harrison)

If you read the credits of George Harrison's 1974 album *Dark Horse*, there are cryptic references to George's wife Pattie and Eric Clapton in the musician credits of George's cover of The Everly Brothers' 'Bye Bye Love'. Rumours are that Clapton himself contributed on guitar with Pattie on backing vocals. They don't. This is an example of Harrison's black humour: Pattie had left him for Clapton earlier that year. Apple Records missed the joke and asked permission from Clapton's record company: 'Eric Clapton appears through the courtesy of RSO Records'...!

The lyrics of 'Bye Bye Love' include the new line 'There goes our lady with a you-know-who, I hope she's happy and old Clapper too.'

Ouch.

Arthur Louis: ***Knocking On Heaven's Door***

Recorded January 1975 at Essex Sound Studios, London. Released August 1975. Highest position: did not chart. Produced by Arthur Louis.

'The Dealer' (Louis)
'Come On And Love Me' (Louis)
'Train 444' (Louis)
'Go Out And Make It Happen' (Louis)
'Plum' (Louis)
'Knockin' On Heaven's Door' (Dylan)

In January 1975, Clapton recorded an album's worth of songs for UK-based reggae singer Arthur Louis. 'The Dealer' features Gene 'Duke of Earl' Chandler on vocals. Eric plays some tasty guitar licks. 'Come And Love Me' is driven by Eric's dirty slide guitar and 'Train 444' has an attractive chord progression, let down by Louis' uncertain vocals. Clapton plays some bubbling wah-wah guitar.

'Go Out And Make It Happen' is an unconvincing attempt at a funky rock song. It does not sound at all like Eric on lead guitar. 'Plum' is an instrumental with some beautiful wah-wah leads – again, it's not really in Eric's style, but it might be him.

The gentle reggae cover of Bob Dylan's 'Knocking on Heaven's Door', on which Eric provides a delicate guitar solo, would be released as a single in July 1975, by which time Clapton had recorded his own version of Louis' arrangement note-for-note for a standalone single. 'Someone Like You', written by Louis, was recorded by Clapton for the b-side. Louis' version of 'Layla' remains unreleased.

The album was remixed and re-released in 1988, giving more prominence to EC's guitar.

Bob Dylan: ***Desire***

Recorded 28 July 1975 at Columbia Studio E, New York. Released January 1976. Highest position: US: 1, UK: 3. Produced by Arthur Louis.

'Romance In Durango' (Dylan, Levy)
'Catfish' (Dylan, Levy)
'Money Blues' (Dylan, Levy)
'One More Cup Of Coffee (Valley Below)' (Dylan)
'Oh, Sister' (Dylan, Levy)
'Hurricane' (Dylan, Levy)

During a three-week break in his 1975 North American tour, Eric took part in a chaotic session in New York for Bob Dylan's *Desire*. Clapton plays on 'Romance in Durango' but you'd be hard-pressed to pick him out. The wonderful, bluesy outtake 'Catfish' released on the third volume of *The Bootleg Series* in 1991, has some very Claptonesque Dobro. This is noted on the session logs as being recorded on 29 July (i.e., the day after the confirmed sessions with Clapton), but listening to the recording strongly suggests it's Eric.

Clinton Heylin notes a further four other unreleased songs from the Dylan/ Clapton sessions. One of these, 'Hurricane', is supposedly included on the bootleg album *Abandoned Desire*, but you can never be certain of these things: Eric might be playing here, but then again…

The others remain unreleased and unheard.

Rick Danko: ***Rick Danko***

Recorded April 1976 at Shangri-La, Malibu. Released January 1977. Highest position: did not chart. Produced by Rick Danko and Rob Fraboni.

'New Mexicoe' (Danko, Charles)

During sessions for *No Reason to Cry* in Malibu, Eric Clapton contributed to three other albums. The typically plaintive 'New Mexicoe' (sic) is from Band bassist Rick Danko's self-titled debut album and features two restrained but melodic electric guitar solos. Eric:

> Rick's singing has had a tremendous influence on me, from 'Big Pink' right up to the present day. It's only my own humble opinion, but I think you have to be a great musician before you can sing like that.

Kinky Friedman: ***Lasso From El Paso***

Recorded April 1976 at Shangri-La, Malibu. Released 1976. Highest position: did not chart. Produced by Kinky Friedman, Huey P. Meaux and Steve Popovich.

'Kinky' (Hawkins)

'Ol' Ben Lucas' (Friedman)

Clapton shreds some fluid Dobro on two songs from Kinky Friedman's *Lasso from El Paso*. Friedman is an acquired taste, for sure: 'Ol' Ben Lucas' celebrates rhinotillexomania. Rick Danko, Levon Helm and Dr. John also play on these songs.

Joe Cocker: ***Stingray***

Recorded April 1976 at Shangri-La, Malibu. Released 1976. Highest position: did not chart. Produced by Kinky Friedman, Huey P. Meaux and Steve Popovich.

'Worrier' (Moore)

Joe Cocker's career started on a high: a number one single with his first release and an appearance at Woodstock. He was a big-name touring act in the early 1970s. By 1976, he was struggling with alcohol and drug problems and was many tens of thousands of dollars in debt.

The slow blues-waltz 'Worrier' has some delicate electric lead work from Clapton. Richard Tee and Steve Gadd play on this richly produced track – both would work on Clapton's solo albums in years to come.

Peter Tosh: ***Legalize It!***

Recorded 1976 at Treasure Isle and Randy's, Kingston, Jamaica. Released 1976. Highest position: did not chart. Produced by Peter Tosh.

'Legalize It!' (Tosh)
'Brand New Second Hand' (Tosh)
'Igiabeher (Let Jah Be Praised)' (Tosh)
'Ketchy Shuby' (Tosh)
'No Sympathy' (Tosh)
'Till Your Well Runs Dry' (Tosh)
'Why Must I Cry' (Tosh, Marley)

Some sources suggest that Eric played on the sessions for Peter Tosh's breakthrough album *Legalize It!* He certainly recorded several of the songs himself for his own albums, but there is no documented proof of his involvement in 1976.

However, the 2011 re-release of *Legalize It!* Includes an 'original Jamaican mix' of 'Till Your Well Runs Dry', which either has Eric's playing or someone doing a very good take-off.

Stephen Bishop: ***Careless***

Recorded June 1976 at ABC Studios / A&M Studios, Los Angeles. Released 1976. Highest position: did not chart. Produced by Henry Lewy and Stephen Bishop.

'Save It For A Rainy Day' (Bishop)
'Sinking In An Ocean Of Tears' (Bishop)

Stephen Bishop's career seems to have been based on having a well-connected address book. The lightweight 'Save It for a Rainy Day' from his debut album *Careless* was a top 30 hit in the US

Eric Clapton plays a very short wah-wah solo on this and is barely audible on 'Sinking in an Ocean of Tears' from the same album.

Ringo Starr: ***Ringo's Rotogravure***

Recorded June 1976 at Cherokee, Los Angeles. Released September 1976. Highest position: US: 28, UK: did not chart. Produced by Arif Mardin.

'This Be Called A Song' (Clapton)

Ringo Starr is one of the greatest rock drummers, but his singing career can be measured by the quality of his collaborators.

'This Be Called A Song' is a rare Clapton original donated to another artist. Clapton adds bluesy lead guitar to this otherwise forgettable track from Ringo's patchy-at-best *Ringo's Rotogravure*.

Corky Laing: ***Makin' It On The Street***

Recorded June 1976 at Westlake Audio, Los Angeles. Released 1976. Highest position: did not chart. Produced by Arif Mardin.

'On My Way (By The River)' (Laing)
Corky Laing was the drummer in the sub-Cream bands Mountain and West, Bruce and Liang. 'On My Way (By the River)' from *Makin' It on The Street* is a one-note shouter that wastes the talents of Eric Clapton, George Terry and Dicky Betts.

The Band: *The Last Waltz*
Recorded November 1976 at Winterland Arena, San Francisco. Released April 1978. Highest chart position: did not chart. Expanded reissue released April 2002. Highest chart position: did not chart. Produced by Robbie Robertson.

'All Our Pastimes' (Clapton, Danko)
'Further on Up the Road' (Robey, Veasey)
'I Shall Be Released' (Dylan)
'Jam #1' (Young, Wood, Clapton, Robertson, Butterfield, Rebennack, Hudson, Danko, Starkey, Helm)
'Jam #2' (Young, Wood, Clapton, Stills, Butterfield, Rebennack, Hudson, Radle, Starr and Helm)
The Band were a huge influence on Eric Clapton's early career, to the degree that he wanted to leave Cream after he heard The Band's debut album. He wrote in his memoirs:

> *Music from Big Pink*... was fantastic. It stopped me in my tracks, and it also highlighted all of the problems I thought we had. Here was a band that was really doing it right, incorporating influences from country music, blues, jazz, and rock, and writing great songs. I couldn't help but compare them to us, which was stupid and futile, but I was frantically looking for a yardstick, and here it was. Listening to that album, as great as it was, just made me feel that we were stuck, and I wanted out.

Clapton's album *No Reason To Cry* was recorded at The Band's Shangri-La Studios. It's no surprise that Clapton was invited to take part in their farewell show towards the end of 1976, along with a host of A-list friends: Bob Dylan, Neil Diamond, Dr. John, Joni Mitchell, Van Morrison, Ringo Starr, Muddy Waters, Ronnie Wood, Neil Young.

The Last Waltz is one of the greatest live albums of all time. A spine-tingling blues section gives us Paul Butterfield blasting harmonica on 'Mystery Train', Muddy Waters stamping his authority on 'Mannish Boy' and Clapton almost dropping his guitar on a ragged but furious version of 'Further On Up The Road'. Everyone sang along on the finale, 'I Shall Be Released'.

An expanded reissue in 2002 adds Eric duetting with Rick Danko on 'All Our Pastimes' – a song they wrote together earlier that year – along with two inessential onstage jams. Note that both of these are heavily edited from their full-length versions available on the bootleg *The Complete Last Waltz*.

Roger Daltrey: ***One Of The Boys***

Recorded January 1977 at Ramport Studios, Battersea, London. Released May 1977. Highest position: US: 46, UK: 45. Produced by Dave Courtney and Tony Meehan.

'Parade' (Goodhand-Tait)
'Single Man's Dilemma' (Blunstone)
'Avenging Annie' (Pratt)
'The Prisoner' (Courtney, Todd, Daltrey)
'Leon' (Goodhand-Tait)
'One of the Boys' (Gibbons)
'Giddy' (McCartney)
'Say It Ain't So, Joe' (Head)
'Written on the Wind' (Korda)
'Satin and Lace' (Courtney, Meehan, Daltrey)
'Doing It All Again' (Courtney, Meehan, Daltrey)
'You Put Something Better Inside Me' (Rafferty, Egan)
'Martyrs and Madmen' (Swindells)
'Treachery' (Swindells)
'Dear John' (Courtney) – b-side of 'Written on the Wind'

Clapton is credited as one of the many guitarists on Roger Daltrey's third solo album *One Of The Boys,* along with Alvin Lee, Jimmy McCulloch, Hank Marvin and Mick Ronson, amongst others. Daltrey described it as 'a poxy, complete piece-of-crap album' in an interview with *Q* magazine.

Clapton archivist Marc Roberty writes, 'although Eric participated in these sessions, it is not known what guitar parts survived. I cannot find any trace of Eric.'

We, therefore, list all of the songs recorded at these sessions on the proviso that Eric might be on none of them. Or all of them.

Pete Townshend and Ronnie Lane: ***Rough Mix***

Recorded February 1977 at Olympic Sound Studios, London. Released September 1977. Highest position: US: 45, UK: 44. Produced by Glyn Johns.

'Rough Mix' (Townshend, Lane)
'Annie' (Lane, Lambert, Clapton)
'April Fool' (Lane)
'Till the Rivers All Run Dry' (Williams, Holyfield)

Rough Mix is a terrific blend of the more rustic music of The Who and The (Small) Faces. Both Pete Townshend and Ronnie Lane had achieved

considerable commercial and critical success since 1965, and this inspired album is relaxed, entertaining and a comfort blanket of great music. Glyn Johns:

> Pete Townshend and Ronnie Lane decided that they wanted to make an album together. They called me up and asked me if I'd like to produce it. I had been really good friends and worked with both of them for years, so it was a no-brainer.

The instrumental title track rocks hard and is the sound of a roomful of musicians delighting in each other's company. Johns:

> Pete had written an instrumental for guitar. He told me that he wanted Eric Clapton to come and play it for the record. I thought this was a terrible idea as I felt that Pete should play his own instrumental; after all, it was his album. I had little time for Eric after the debacle of his [Rainbow] concert and his not showing up at the studio to fix his performance. I thought that we could do without the negative energy that I associated with him at that time. Pete insisted and told me in no uncertain terms that there was no conversation. He was not going to play it and Eric was, as he had written it specifically for him. I agreed as it seemed that I had no option. I figured I could put up with the rather sour presence of Eric for an afternoon. Well, I could not have been more wrong. We started the session at 2:30 p.m. Eric was on time and learned the piece really quickly and we had the track finished in no time. The whole experience being totally different than I had predicted. He was together and perfectly pleasant to work with.

Clapton adds acoustic guitar and/or Dobro to Ronnie Lane's gorgeous ballads 'Annie' (co-written by Clapton) and 'April Fool'. Johns, again:

> A few days later, [Eric] swung by the studio to see how we were doing. We had just finished a song called 'April Fool'. Ronnie had done a wonderful vocal ... and all we had left to do was the solo. We all thought a Dobro would be a great sound to complement what we had done, and Eric offered to play it. There are a few moments in my recording career that I treasure and this is one of them. I played him the track and I noticed that his foot was tapping as he ran through the song. I quickly put a mic on his foot and we recorded the next run-through. It was note-perfect and quite beautiful. Eric reacting in the most natural and emotive way to the song and Ronnie's performance of it. Up until that moment I had paid very little attention to Eric as a musician and, therefore, never really understood what all the fuss was about. I thought he was just another bloody white kid playing the blues. That was very clearly my loss. In a matter of a few minutes, I had been completely won over. This was a perfect example of what I have always thought since about Eric's playing. He never allows his brain to get in the way between his heart and his fingers.

Best of all, Clapton provides superbly melodic Dobro to a dead-straight cover of Don Williams' country hit 'Till the Rivers All Run Dry'.

Johns would work with Clapton on his next album, *Slowhand*, recorded at Olympic three months later and on several others.

Ijahman Levi: ***Haile I Hymn***
Ijahman Levi: ***Are We A Warrior***

Recorded December 1977 at Joe Gibbs Studio, Kingston, Jamaica. ***Haile I Hymn*** released 1978. Highest position: did not chart. ***Are We A Warrior*** released 1979. Highest position: did not chart. Produced by Ijahman Levi.

'Jah Heavy Load' (Sutherland)
'Jah Is No Secret' (Sutherland)
'Zion Hut' (Sutherland)
'I'm A Levi' (Sutherland)
'Are We A Warrior' (Sutherland)
'Moulding' (Sutherland)
'The Church' (Sutherland)
'Miss Beverly' (Sutherland)
'Two Sides Of Love' (Sutherland)

Late in 1977, Clapton took part in sessions in London for reggae artist Ijahman Levi but his contributions to *Haile I Hymn* (1978) and *Are we a Warrior* (1979) are not obviously audible.

White Mansions: ***White Mansions***

Recorded January 1978 at Olympic Sound Studios, London. Released June 1978. Highest position: did not chart. Produced by Glyn Johns.

'White Trash' (Kennerley, Leadon)
'Kentucky Racehorse' (Kennerley)

The ambitious *White Mansions* project documents the lives of American southerners in the Confederacy during the American Civil War of 1861-1865. It was produced by Glyn Johns at Olympic in January 1978, with songs written by Paul Kennerley and sung by Waylon Jennings, Jessi Colter, John Dillon and Steve Cash. Clapton plays gutsy electric slide on 'White Trash' and subtle Dobro on 'Last Dance and the Kentucky Racehorse'. It's a fascinating album that doesn't quite hold together.

Alexis Korner: ***The Party Album***

Recorded April 1978 at The Gatsby Room, Pinewood Studios, Iver Heath, Buckinghamshire. Released 1980. Highest position: did not chart. Produced by Alexis Korner.

'Hey Pretty Mama' (Farlowe)
'Hi-Heel Sneakers' (Higginbotham)
'Stormy Monday Blues' (Eckstein, Hines)

Whilst we can sit back and appreciate the influence that Alexis Korner had on the post-war British blues scene, it's hard to forgive the release of this horrendous live album. It had been filmed and recorded at Pinewood Studios for a BBC documentary but remained in the can for two years. It should have stayed there.

On paper, the band is top-notch: Korner, Zoot Money, Mel Collins, Dick Heckstall-Smith, Dick Morrissey, Chris Farlowe, Colin Hodgkinson and others. Describing their performances as 'loose' would be generous – Eric busks along on three tired and emotional twelve-bar blues.

A fourth performance with Eric, 'Can't Get You Out Of My Mind', remains unreleased.

George Harrison: *George Harrison*

Recorded December 1978 at FPSHOT, Henley-on-Thames. Released February 1979. Highest position: US: 14, UK: 39. Produced by George Harrison and Russ Titelman.

'Love Comes To Everyone' (Harrison)

George Harrison's eighth solo album dates from several sessions across 1978. Eric adds stinging lead guitar to the slick MOR track 'Love Comes to Everyone'. Steve Winwood provides a distinctive Polymoog break. Eric recorded the song himself for *Back Home*, released in 2005, as a tribute to his old friend.

Marc Benno: *Lost In Austin*

Recorded January 1979 at Olympic Sound Studios, London. Released June 1979. Highest position: did not chart. Produced by Glyn Johns.

'Hotfoot Blues' (Benno)
'Chasin' Rainbows' (Benno)
'Me And A Friend Of Mine' (Benno)
'New Romance' (Benno)
'Last Train' (Benno)
'Lost In Austin' (Benno)
'Splish Splash' (Darin, Kaufman)
'Monterrey Pen' (Benno)
'The Drifter' (Benno)
'Hey There Senorita' (Benno)

Dallas-born singer-songwriter Marc Benno has flown under the radar for fifty years. His partnership with Leon Russell in The Asylum Choir kickstarted both of their careers. Benno recorded four albums for A&M Records in Hollywood in the 1970s and, in between, he played on four tracks for The Doors' *L.A. Woman*.

Lost in Austin is a loose and gently entertaining album which sits in a space surrounded by J.J. Cale, Tom Waits, Arlo Guthrie and Dr. John. It was recorded at Olympic in January 1979 and features Clapton with Albert Lee and his Tulsa rhythm section on every track.

The opening 'Hotfoot Blues' is a deliciously loose shuffle, with Benno's idiosyncratic vocals and Clapton's colourful slide guitar. 'Chasin' Rainbows' is a delightful acoustic track which could have come straight off a Ronnie Lane album. Eric deploys his lovely Dobro tones and producer Glyn Johns embellishes the track with tasteful strings. 'Me And A Friend Of Mine' could be an *Okie* outtake – Eric's solo is pure J. J. Cale. Piano, organ and strings underpin the slow 'New Romance'. Clapton's contribution is not obvious: he's either mixed low or not involved. In contrast, Eric is all over 'Last Train' with some thrilling lead guitar lines from the opening note and a very fluid solo. The album's highlight is 'Lost In Austin', a wry song with clever lyrics, descending arpeggios and a lush production. Eric plays opulent Dobro. The cover of Bobby Darin's 'Splish Splash' is fun but inessential. Eric sticks to rhythm. 'Monterrey Pen' is another J. J. Cale reprint, with some fabulous EC guitar licks and a beautiful lyrical solo which lifts the track immeasurably. Finally, 'The Drifter' replicates Leon Russell's voodoo groove with some sharp electric lead breaks, and 'Hey There Senorita' is a back-porch strum-along with an acoustic guitar solo which is right in Eric's style but might be Albert Lee. All-in-all, *Lost In Austin* is an excellent album that fans of Clapton's 1970s work are encouraged to track down.

Danny Douma: *Night Eyes*

Recorded March 1979 Village Recorder, Los Angeles. Released 1979. Highest position: did not chart. Produced by Danny Douma and Nick van Maarth.

'Hate You' (Douma)

Former Big Wha-Koo singer and guitarist Danny Douma signed a management contract with Mick Fleetwood in 1978. Douma's debut solo album *Night Eyes,* recorded in Los Angeles in March 1979, has the killer Mick Fleetwood / John McVie / Christine McVie rhythm section and, on the bluesy laid-back shuffle 'Hate You', some sweet Dobro and liquid electric lead by Eric Clapton. The album was co-produced by Douma with his former Big Wha-Koo bandmate Nick van Maarth.

Douma toured with Fleetwood Mac as a supporting act for the remainder of 1979 but was unable to find commercial success.

The 1980s

Clapton started the 1980s at a career low, but ended them as an elder statesman of pop. In between this renaissance he played some of his best session work – see Roger Waters, Gary Brooker, Jack Bruce, George Harrison – and also some of his worst, with by-the-numbers solos for Lionel Richie, Tina Turner and, yes, Davina McCall.

At least he stayed interesting…

Ronnie Lane: *See Me*

Recorded January 1980 at LMS Mobile Recording Studio and Marcus Recording Studios. Released 1980. Did not chart. Produced by Bob Potter.

'Lad's Got Money' (Lane)
'Barcelona' (Lane, Clapton)
'Way Up Yonder' (traditional)

See Me was Ronnie Lane's fourth and last solo album. He had been diagnosed with multiple sclerosis in 1977 and would struggle with ill-health until his death in 1997. 'Lad's Got Money' (or 'When Lad Has Money' on the original album's insert) is a rolling waltz-time Lane song with a short, taut guitar solo; 'Barcelona' is a gorgeous Lane/Clapton co-write with tasteful bluesy leads and what sounds like Eric on nylon-strung acoustic; 'Way Up Yonder' is a short, light-hearted arrangement of the old gospel/bluegrass song 'Will The Angels Play Their Harps For Me?'. Clapton is, unfortunately, inaudible.

Gary Brooker: 'Leave The Candle' / 'Chasing The Chop'

Recorded March 1980 at Surrey Sound Studios, Leatherhead. Released April 1981. Did not chart. Produced by Gary Brooker.

'Leave The Candle' (Brooker, Sinfield)
'Chasing The Chop' (Brooker, Reid)

The Gary Brooker single 'Leave The Candle', backed with 'Chasing The Chop', dates from Surrey Sound in Leatherhead, around the time that Brooker joined Clapton's band in early 1980.

'Leave The Candle' is one of the few songs included in this book that has never been re-issued digitally – if you want to hear it, then, like me, you need to head to eBay and buy the original 7" single. It's a lovely, commercial country-tinged track with a great Brooker vocal and some delightful picking from Eric, very much in his *Slowhand* / *Backless* style. It's a crying shame that this has not been more widely heard.

'Chasing The Chop' starts as a simple piano boogie but kicks into gear with a strong chorus and a driving guitar solo from Clapton. He also plays some low-in-the-mix Dobro. Note that different pressings give this song slightly different names: it's 'Chasing The Chop' on Charisma CHS 2396, but 'Chasing For The

Above: Eric, not in the best of health, performs at rock's first big charity show, the Concert for Bangladesh, in 1971.

Above: Clapton has long supported the Prince's Trust. Here he is performing in 2010 with Mark King and Jools Holland. Phil Collins is just out of shot.

Left: Aretha Franklin: *Lady Soul* (1968). Eric Clapton's first American guest recording session, recorded at Atlantic Studios, New York during sessions for Cream's *Wheels Of Fire*. (*Atlantic / Warner Music Group*)

Right: The Mothers Of Invention: *We're Only In It For The Money* (1968). Eric Clapton appears on two songs, 'Are You Hung Up?' and on 'Nasal Retentive Calliope Music'. (*Verve / Universal Music Group*)

Left: Howlin' Wolf: *The London Howlin' Wolf Sessions* (1971). Clapton and heavy friends back up Howlin' Wolf to scintillating effect. (*Chess / Universal Music Group*)

Right: Dr John: *Sun Moon & Herbs (*1971). Dr. John's music irresistibly combines blues, pop, jazz, boogie-woogie, funk and rock and roll. Clapton is credited as guitarist on all tracks on his fourth album. (*Atlantic / Warner Music Group*)

Left: James Luther Dickinson: *Dixie Fried* (1972). Recorded during sessions for Buddy Guy's and Junior Wells' *Play The Blues*, with some of the same musicians and producer. (*Atlantic / Warner Music Group*)

Right: John Mayall: *Back To The Roots* (1971). Eric plays some trebly guitar on several tracks on John Mayall's 1971 album. (*Polydor / Universal Music Group*)

Left: Various Artists: *The Concert For Bangla-desh* (1972). The first big-name rock benefit show. A number one album in the UK and the US and winner of the Grammy for Album of the Year at the 1973 awards. (*Apple / Universal Music Group*)

Right: Bob Dylan: *Desire* (1976). Clapton plays on 'Romance in Durango', but you'd be hard-pressed to pick him out. The wonderful, bluesy outtake 'Catfish' has some very Claptonesque Dobro, however. (*CBS / Sony Music Entertainment*)

Left: Roger Daltrey: *One Of The Boys* (1977). Clapton is credited as one of the many guitarists on Roger Daltrey's third solo album. Daltrey himself described it as 'a poxy, complete piece-of-crap album'. (*MCA / Universal Music Group*)

Right: Townshend Lane: *Rough Mix* (1977). The album is a terrific blend of the more rustic music of The Who and The (Small) Faces. It's wonderful from start to finish. (*MCA / Universal Music Group*)

Left: Ronnie Lane: *See Me* (1980). This is Ronnie Lane's fourth and last solo album. 'Barcelona' is a gorgeous Lane/Clapton co-write with tasteful bluesy leads and what sounds like Eric on nylon-strung acoustic. (*CBS / Sony Music Entertainment*)

Right: Stephen Bishop: *Red Cab To Manhattan* (1980). Eric plays on two songs on Stephen Bishop's third album recorded at Air Studios in London in March 1980. (*Warner Bros / Warner Music Group*)

Left: Phil Collins: *Face Value* (1981). 'If Leaving Me Is Easy' is typical of Phil Collins' low-key, very personal and often heart-breaking first solo album. Eric's playing is inaudible, but the demo, released in 2020, has unmistakable and delicately picked Clapton lead guitar lines. (*Virgin / Sony Music Entertainment*)

Right: Various Artists: *Secret Policeman's Other Ball – The Music*. Eric is outshined by Jeff Beck at this charity show for Amnesty International. (*Island / Universal Music Group*)

Left: Ringo Starr: *Old Wave* (1983). 'Everybody's In A Hurry But Me' knocks off the Bo Diddley beat and is co-credited to Ringo, Joe Walsh, John Entwistle, Eric Clapton and Chris Stainton: a lot of talent for a slight one chord jam and a single spoken line of vocals. (*Bellaphon*)

Right: Christine McVie: *Christine McVie* (1984). Eric's solo on 'The Challenge' has a light touch that suits the song perfectly. (*Warner Bros / Warner Music Group*)

Left: Roger Waters: *The Pros and Cons of Hitch Hiking* (1984). Clapton's work on Roger Waters' first post-Floyd album is nothing short of revelatory. In particular, '4:41AM (Sexual Revolution)' has some exceptional lead guitar. (*EMI / Sony Music Entertainment*)

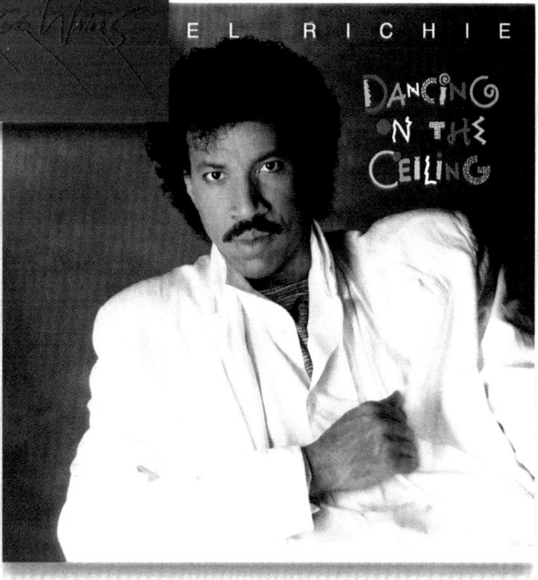

Right: Lionel Richie: *Dancing On The Ceiling* (1986). 'Tonight Will Be Alright' is a typical mid-80s AOR mid-tempo album filler. Eric's solos are very short and stick to his usual style. (*Motown / Universal Music Group*)

Left: George Harrison: *Cloud Nine* (1987). Eric plays on four songs on George Harrison's triumphant 1987 album. (*Dark Horse / BMG)*

Right: Jim Capaldi: *Some Come Running* (1988). The ex-Traffic singer/drummer recruited many famous friends for this album, including Eric Clapton, Steve Winwood and George Harrison. (*Island / Universal Music Group*)

Left: Carole King: *City Streets* (1989). Unfortunately, Carole King's 1989 album suffers from sludgy 1980s production. King's singing is terrific, though. Clapton plays on two songs. (*Capitol / Universal Music Group*)

Right: Cyndi Lauper: *A Night To Remember* (1989). Cyndi Lauper and Eric Clapton are perhaps unlikely musical partners. How much you enjoy Eric's contribution to 'Insecurious' depends on your opinion of the Brooklynite. (*Epic / Sony Music Entertainment*)

Left: Kate Bush: *The Red Shoes* (1993). Eric Clapton plays some powerful, punchy blues riffs on 'And So Is Love', one of his best sessions for another artist. (*EMI / Universal Music Group*)

Right: Johnnie Johnson: *Johnnie B. Bad* (1991). Eric plays on two tracks on this solo album by Chuck Berry's piano player. (*Elektra / Warner Music Group*)

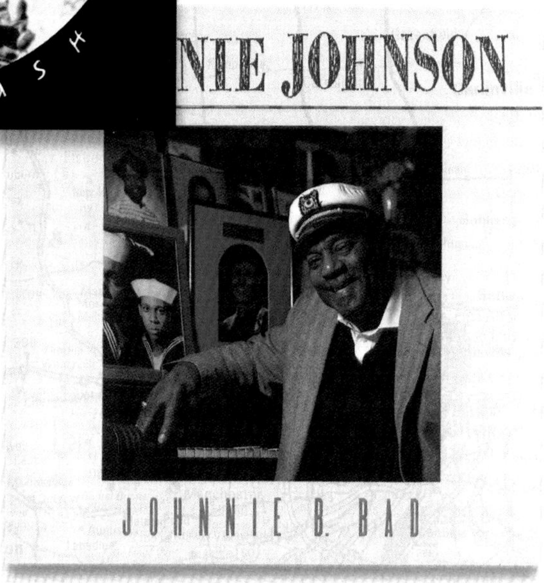

Left: Richie Sambora: *Stranger In This Town* (1991). Eric plays on 'Mr Bluesman', an unsubtle tribute to Clapton by the Bon Jovi guitarist. (*Mercury Records / Universal Music Group*)

Right: Babyface: *The Day* (1996). Babyface's fourth album. Eric Clapton plays some delicate electric guitar leads on the song 'Talk To Me'. (*Epic / Sony Music Entertainment*)

Left: BB King: *Deuces Wild* (1997). Eric plays and sings on a new version of King's 1964 hit single 'Rock Me Baby'. They work well together in an irresistible combination. (*MCA / Universal Music Group*)

Right: Bill Wyman's Rhythm Kings: *Struttin' Our Stuff* (1998). Eric busks along and drops a tight, trebly solo on a version of The Rolling Stones' 'Melody'. (*Velvel*)

Left: Original Soundtrack: *Blues Brothers 2000* (1998). I tried to pretend that this doesn't exist. For completists only. (*Universal Records / Universal Music Group*)

Right: Mary J Blige: *Mary* (1999). 'Give Me You' is a torch ballad, uplifting and strong despite Diane Warren's trademark trucker's modulation. There is no guitar solo as such but Eric adds some thick Ernie Isley riffs to the chorus. (*MCA / Universal Music Group*)

Left: Tony Rich Project: *Birdseye* (1998). The Tony Rich Project mixes acoustic, folk-flavoured pop with modern soul. Think of Stevie Wonder and Marvin Gaye distilled through D'Angelo and Babyface with a nineties production. (*La Face Records / BMG*)

Right: Santana: *Supernatural* (1999). 'The Calling', eight minutes in length, starts as a slow, moody guitar duet. The pace picks up and the two men exchange powerful guitar phrases to a vocal refrain. (*Arista / Sony Music Entertainment*)

Left: Paul McCartney: *Driving Rain* (2001). 'Freedom' was written in response to the 11 September attacks in 2001 and was performed at the Concert For New York City on 20 October 2001 with Eric on lead guitar. (*Parlophone / Warner Music Group*)

Right: Brian Wilson: *Gettin' In Over My Head* (2004). 'City Blues' allows Eric to add some loud but generic lead guitar. (*Rhino-East West / Warner Music Group*)

Left: Ringo Starr: *Ringo Rama* (2003). It's wholly appropriate that Eric contributed to Ringo Starr's moving tribute to George Harrison with 'Never Without You'. Eric's solo is edgy and liquid. (*KOCH Records / MNRK Music Group*)

Right: Buddy Guy: *Blues Singer* (2003). This acoustic version of John Lee Hooker's 'Crawling King Snake' is transcendent, with both Clapton and B. B. King adding their unmistakable guitar styles to a superb track. (*Silvertone / Sony Music UK*)

Left: Bruce Hornsby: *Halcyon Days* (2004). Bruce Hornsby's solo career contains many intriguing albums which are difficult to classify but easy to enjoy. The lethargic but atmospheric 'Halcyon Days' is a Sting / Hornsby duet. Clapton adds a short, delicate, gorgeous solo. It's one of his best. (*Columbia / Sony Music Entertainment*)

Right: Marcus Miller: *Silver Rain* (2005). This smooth funk/reggae track, suits Clapton like a Versace whistle. His singing, sometimes overlooked due to his prowess on the guitar, is wonderful. (*KOCH Records / MNRK Music Group*)

Left: Steve Winwood: *Nine Lives* (2008). Eric Clapton adds some loud, gritty guitar to the eight-minute 'Dirty City', which revisits the slinky funk-rock crossover of early Traffic. (*Columbia / Sony Music Entertainment*)

Right: Buddy Guy: *Skin Deep* (2008). Both Buddy Guy and Eric Clapton sing and play superbly, absolutely in sync with each other – Clapton has some real grit in his throat and stretches out with some dynamic soloing. (*Silvertone / Sony Music UK*)

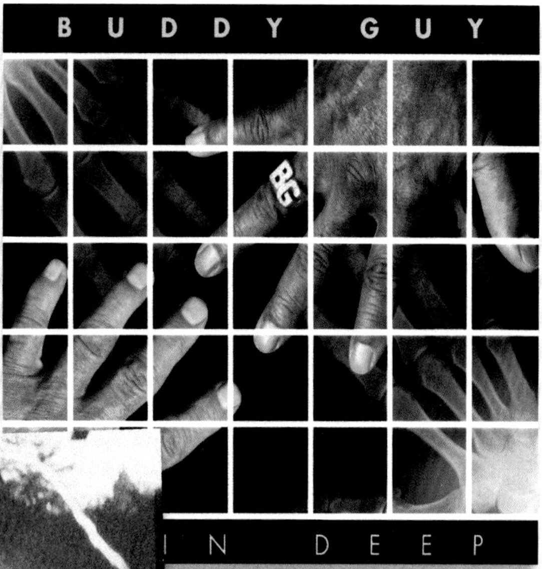

Left: Robbie Robertson: *How To Become Clairvoyant* (2011). Clapton plays on seven tracks, sings on one, co-writes two and – unusually – donates a song. (*Macrobiotic Records*)

Right: Jerry Douglas: *Traveler* (2012). Clapton sings a duet with Jerry Douglas. The first guitar solo is pure Douglas, the second is classic Clapton – slow, easy, magnificent. (*eOne Music / MNRK Music Group*)

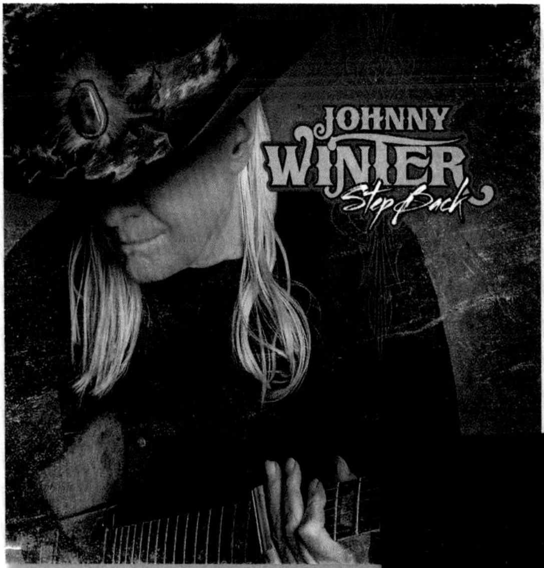

Left: Johnny Winter: *Step Back* (2014). The cover of Don Robey's 'Don't Want No Woman' features Johnny Winter and Eric Clapton trading guitar licks – in truth, Clapton doesn't sound wholly engaged and Winter takes the musical garlands. (*Megaforce Records*)

Right: Nathan East: *Nathan East* (2014). Nathan East has appeared on more than 2,000 albums over the past 35 years. His debut solo album includes a classy version of Blind Faith's 'Can't Find My Way Home'. Clapton is all over it. (*Yamaha Music Communications*)

Left: Ed Sheeran: *Divide* (2017). Eric is credited as Angelo Mysterioso on 'Dive'. The pseudonym was first used by George Harrison on Cream's *Goodbye*, recorded 22 years before Ed Sheeran was born. (*Asylum / Warner Music Group*)

Chop' on the b-side of the Phonogram single 'Homelovin'' (1981). The song can be heard on the CD reissue of 1982's *Lead Me To The Water.*

Stephen Bishop: ***Red Cab To Manhattan***

Recorded March 1980 at Air Studios, London. Released 1980. Did not chart. Produced by Mike Mainieri and Tommy LiPuma.

'Little Moon' (Bishop)

'Sex Kittens Go To College' (Bishop)

Eric plays on two songs on Stephen Bishop's third album *Red Cab To Manhattan*, recorded at Air Studios in London in March 1980. 'Little Moon' is a slow piano ballad that switches half-way to a blatant Billy Joel facsimile. Eric's contribution is minimal. 'Sex Kittens Go To College' has some great lead guitar breaks, but this is a jokey song that fails to be funny. Thankfully, it's very short. Phil Collins was the drummer on these sessions and this marks the first time that he played professionally with Eric Clapton.

Gary Brooker: ***Lead Me To The Water***

Recorded July 1980 at Compass Point Studios, Nassau. Released January 1982. Did not chart. Produced by Tom Dowd.

'Lead Me To The Water' (Brooker)

'Home Lovin'' (Brooker)

Gary Brooker was a member of Eric Clapton's touring band when these two tracks were recorded during the sessions for Clapton's *Another Ticket* album. 'Home Lovin'' features some great lead work from Eric. 'Lead Me To The Water' is a tired reggae with Clapton playing chugging rhythm guitar. Both can be heard on 1982's *Lead Me To The Water* (along with 'Chasing The Chop' on the CD reissue only).

Phil Collins: ***Face Value***

Phil Collins: ***Face Value (expanded version)***

Phil Collins: ***Other Sides***

Recorded November 1980 at the Townhouse in London. ***Face Value*** released February 1981. Highest chart positions: US: 7, UK: 1. ***Face Value (expanded version)*** released January 2016. Highest chart positions: UK: 47. ***Other Sides*** released December 2020. Produced by Phil Collins and Hugh Padgham.

'If Leaving Me Is Easy' (Collins)

'If Leaving Me Is Easy (demo)' (Collins)

'The Roof Is Leaking (demo)' (Collins)

As 1980 turned into 1981, Phil Collins was about to embark on a remarkable career rebirth. Collins had joined the band Genesis in mid-1970, just as their star began to rise. 1971's *Nursery Cryme* entered the UK top forty and heralded a golden period with *Foxtrot* and *Selling England By The Pound* both reaching the top twenty. Collins sang lead vocals on 'For Absent Friends' and 'More Fool Me' but wasn't the obvious choice as a new lead singer and frontman to replace Peter Gabriel, who left Genesis in 1975. Under Collins' guidance, they would have a run of five number one albums between 1980 and 1991. Risking commercial ubiquity, Collins commenced a solo career with 'In The Air Tonight', released as a single on 5 January 1981 and the album *Face Value* which followed six weeks later.

Collins had met Eric Clapton a couple of years before, as he recalls:

> Our introduction went like this: John [Martyn] has played with Eric and knows him well. One tiring day during the *Grace & Danger* sessions [which Collins produced], he's looking for something to, ah, brighten up his day and thinks Eric can help. So John calls and asks if the pair of us can come over to Eric's house in Ewhurst, not far from The Farm [Genesis' studio]. Eric must have said no—John is the kind of chap who has a tendency to overstay his welcome, and here he's suggesting popping down to score with me, a complete stranger. So we meet in a pub in Guildford. Eric doesn't know me from a bar of soap, but I do remember sitting with a pint of Guinness opposite one of my heroes. Me, quaffing pints in the pub with the guy I'd idolized at the Marquee... Unfortunately, for a while thereafter, I fear that Eric assumes I'm just someone who hangs about with John when he's shopping for drugs. But by the end of '79, Eric and I are very close. By the time [Genesis' album *Duke*] is released, on March 28, 1980, we've already started the tour. That particular day, the middle of three nights at London's Hammersmith Odeon, is when Eric Clapton finally realizes I'm more than a pool-playing drinking pal. He actually sees that I'm a fellow musician, a revelation about which I later hear he's a little surprised.

Later that year, Eric was invited to play guitar on *Face Value*. 'If Leaving Me Is Easy' is typical of Collins' low-key, very personal and often heart-breaking first solo album. Eric's playing is inaudible. 'If Leaving Me Is Easy' was released as the third single from the album and reached number seventeen in the UK.

Face Value was a massive success. It would reach number one in the UK on the week of its release and spent 270 weeks (over five years) in the British album charts that decade. It was also a top tenner in the US

The 2016 expanded re-release of *Face Value* includes a demo version of 'The Roof Is Leaking'. This is ladeled with Clapton's toothsome Dobro. Finally, in late 2020 Collins released the digital-only album *Other Sides.* This includes a demo of 'If Leaving Me Is Easy', which has unmistakable delicately picked Eric Clapton lead guitar lines.

John Martyn: *Glorious Fool*

Recorded February 1981 at the Townhouse in London. Released September 1981. Highest chart positions: US: did not chart, UK: 25. Produced by Phil Collins.

'Couldn't Love You More' (Martyn)
By 1981, the mercurial John Martyn had released eleven albums. Some of these – *Live In London*, *Solid Air* and *One World* – border on genius. At its best, Martyn's music has a wholly original and idiosyncratic sound: gruff vocals and acoustic guitar acrobatics. Eric Clapton's cover of Martyn's 'May You Never' earned him considerable royalties. When Martyn was awarded a BBC Radio 2 Folk Award in 2008, Clapton said:

> John Martyn is so far ahead of everything, it's almost inconceivable.

Adam Sweeting, writing in *The Guardian* in 2009:

> Dabblings with heroin and an American tour with Clapton took Martyn to the brink. He split up with [folk-singer wife] Beverley and made the infamously bleak break-up album *Grace and Danger* (1980) with help from Phil Collins.

Collins:

> I fall in love with John and his music during these sessions. He and I seem to musically hit it off. I go on the road with John and the same guys that made the record. For me, at this time, it's a wonderful release. It's rejuvenating, not least because it's a million miles from the juggernaut that is Genesis. We have great fun, perhaps sometimes too much fun. ... for those of us working close to him, it seems like he's hell-bent on self-destruction. And you can't help but be somewhat dragged in.

Collins produced Martyn's next album, *Glorious Fool* and Eric Clapton plays on 'Couldn't Love You More', first recorded in 1977 for Martyn's incomparable *One World*. It's a long, aching moan of a song, re-recorded with a fuller arrangement for *Glorious Fool*. It's impossible to improve on the original. Eric does, however, add some tasteful lead breaks and a lovely solo to this 1981 arrangement.

Various Artists: ***Secret Policeman's Other Ball – The Music***
Recorded September 1981 at the Theatre Royal, Drury Lane, London. Released March 1982. Highest chart positions: did not chart. Produced by Martin Lewis.

''Cause We Ended As Lovers' (Wonder)
'Further Up The Road' (Robey, Veasey)
'Crossroads' (Johnson)
'I Shall Be Released' (Dylan)
The Secret Policeman's Other Ball was a benefit show staged by the British Section of Amnesty International to raise funds for its research and campaign work. It was directed by John Cleese and took place at the Theatre Royal in

London on 9 September 1981. There were many comedy sketches by the likes of Rowan Atkinson, Alan Bennett, John Bird, Tim Brooke-Taylor, Jasper Carrott, Graham Chapman, Billy Connolly, John Fortune, Barry Humphries, Neil Innes, Chris Langham, Griff Rhys Jones, Alexei Sayle, Pamela Stephenson, John Wells and Victoria Wood, with music by Sting (his first solo performance), Phil Collins, Tom Robinson, Pete Townshend, Bob Geldof and Donovan. Eric Clapton and Jeff Beck performed three songs together — John Cleese introduces them as 'Jeff Beck and Eric Clacton'.

There are good guitarists. There are great guitarists. And then there's Jeff Beck. Clapton plays well, but Beck outshines him all the way here. Stevie Wonder's ''Cause We Ended As Lovers' was recorded by Beck for 1975's *Blow By Blow*. Eric stands back and watches in amazement at Beck's performance here, simply adding a simple strummed accompaniment. They trade blues licks in another version of 'Further Up The Road'. Clapton throws up his hand in submission after Beck's amazing solo. A fiery 'Crossroads' concludes the set.

Clapton joins the all-hands-on-deck finale of 'I Shall Be Released'.

Ringo Starr: *Old Wave*

Recorded December 1981 at the Startling Studios, Ascot. Released June 1983. Highest chart positions: did not chart. Produced by Joe Walsh and Russ Ballard.

'Everybody's In A Hurry But Me' (Starkey, Walsh, Entwistle, Clapton, Stainton)

Eric contributes to Ringo Starr's dismal *Old Wave* album. The song 'Everybody's In A Hurry But Me' knocks off the Bo Diddley beat and is co-credited to Ringo, Joe Walsh, John Entwistle, Eric Clapton and Chris Stainton: a lot of talent for a slight one chord jam and a single spoken line of vocals. This shameful dirge was recorded at Ringo's home studios at Tittenhurst Park in December 1981.

Christine McVie: *Christine McVie*

Recorded January 1983 at Olympic Sound Studios, Barnes. Released 1984. Highest chart positions: UK: 58, US: 26. Produced by Russ Titelman.

'The Challenge' (McVie, Sharp)

The upbeat 'The Challenge' is from Christine McVie's self-titled solo album, recorded at Olympic in June 1983. Eric plays familiar lead breaks – almost as a duet with McVie. His solo is distinctive, with a light touch that suits the song perfectly. The snappy drumming is by future Clapton band member Steve Ferrone.

Corey Hart: *First Offence*

Recorded spring 1983 (probably) at Eel Pie Studios, London. Released November 1983. Highest chart positions: US: 31, UK: did not chart. Produced by Jon Astley and Phil Chapman.

'Jenney Fey' (Hart)

Canadian singer-songwriter Corey Hart released his debut album *First Offence* in November 1983. Eric plays a sweet Dobro solo on the closing 'Jenney Fey', a song which could have come straight from *Face Value* or *Red Cab To Manhattan*. As Hart told *Georgia Straight* in May 1984:

> Jon [Astley, producer] felt there was one song Eric Clapton would really like. So just out of the blue, he sent him the song, and lo and behold, Eric Clapton was on the phone saying he wanted to play on it and asking how I would mind if he did. I didn't. Eric was the classic gentleman. Here I was, this Canadian kid in England with big-time producers doing my first album and Clapton tells me, 'It's such a pretty song, so easy to play. The type of thing I'd write myself'.

Corey Hart has subsequently sold over 16 million records worldwide, including nine consecutive US *Billboard* Top 40 Hits.

Roberty places these sessions in February 1984.

Roger Waters: ***The Pros and Cons of Hitch Hiking***

Recorded August 1983 at The Billiard Room, Barnes (Waters' home studio); Eel Pie Studios, London; Olympic Sound Studios, Barnes. Released April 1984. Highest chart positions: US: 31, UK: 13. Produced by Roger Waters and Michael Kamen.

'4:30AM (Apparently They Were Travelling Abroad)' (Waters)
'4:33AM (Running Shoes)' (Waters)
'4:37AM (Arabs with Knives and West German Skies)' (Waters)
'4:39AM (For the First Time Today, Part 2)' (Waters)
'4:41AM (Sexual Revolution)' (Waters)
'4:47AM (The Remains of Our Love)' (Waters)
'4:50AM (Go Fishing)' (Waters)
'4:56AM (For the First Time Today, Part 1)' (Waters)
'4:58AM (Dunroamin, Duncarin, Dunlivin)' (Waters)
'5:01AM (The Pros and Cons of Hitch Hiking)' (Waters)
'5:06AM (Every Stranger's Eyes)' (Waters)
'5:11AM (The Moment of Clarity)' (Waters)
'5:01AM (The Pros and Cons of Hitch Hiking) – 12" mix' (Waters)

In a move that surprised many, Eric not only performed on Pink Floyd frontman Roger Waters' first official solo album but joined him on tour as well. Recorded in August 1983, Clapton's work on *The Pros and Cons of Hitch Hiking* is nothing short of revelatory. Michael Kamen, who played keyboards on the album:

> Roger was directing Eric back to what he did best. It was a horrible syrupy time for pop music at that point... And Eric, like most vital pop stars, was looking

for this place in that market. What Roger succeeded in doing was getting Eric to refocus on the blues and on one particular track, 'Sexual Revolution', Eric played great blues. He was especially pleased with his playing on that track and actually said, 'You know, I think that's the best I've ever played on a record'.

It's difficult to disagree, even if the album as a whole is not always an easy listen. '4:41AM (Sexual Revolution)' has some exceptional lead guitar if you can get past Waters' strangled bark and sixth-form lyrics. The title track has an eviscerating solo – the 12" version has a different, even better, lead break from Clapton. He sprays dirty licks all over '4:58AM (Dunroamin, Duncarin, Dunlivin)' and '5:06AM (Every Stranger's Eyes)' and breaks out his Dobro on '4:50AM (Go Fishing)'. Despite personal friction with his employer, Clapton toured with Waters in June and July 1984, adding some astonishing solos to Pink Floyd songs such as 'Money', 'If' and 'The Gunner's Dream'. Please track down the soundboard recording from Chicago to understand what all the fuss was about.

Stephen Bishop: *Bowling in Paris*

Recorded April 1984 at Air Studios, Montserrat. Released January 1989. Highest chart positions: did not chart. Produced by Phil Collins, Nick Launay and Michael Omartian.

'Hall Light' (Bishop)

Stephen Bishop's 'Hall Light' features Phil Collins on drums, Eric Clapton on solo guitar and Sting on bass and harmony vocals. Recorded in spring 1984 amid sessions for Clapton's *Behind The Sun* album, it was released on *Bowling in Paris* in 1989. 'Hall Light' is lightweight AOR.

Gary Brooker: *Echoes In The Night*

Recorded January 1985 at Jacobs Studios, Farnham. Released 1985. Highest chart positions: did not chart. Produced by Matthew Fisher and Gary Brooker.

'Echoes In The Night' (Brooker, Fisher, Reid)

Eric Clapton and Gary Brooker were old mates and neighbours: Brooker played Clapton's band between 1980 and 1982, and Eric has played on many of Brooker's charity concerts over the years.

In early 1985, with his playing back at its peak, Clapton added some strong lead guitar licks and a tough solo to the title track to Brooker's *Echoes In The Night*.

Lionel Richie: *Dancing On The Ceiling*

Recorded July 1985 at Bear Creek Recording Studios, Washington. Released August 1986. Highest chart positions: UK: 2, US: 1. Produced by Lionel Richie and James Anthony Carmichael.

'Tonight Will Be Alright' (Richie)
Dancing on the Ceiling is the third and most successful solo studio album by ex-Commodores vocalist Lionel Richie. Released in August 1986, it has sold over four million copies in the US alone. 'Tonight Will Be Alright' is a typical mid-80s AOR mid-tempo album filler. It's not particularly memorable. Eric's solos are very short and stick to his usual style.

Paul Brady: ***Back To The Centre***
Recorded November 1985 at Utopia Sound Studios, London. Released 1986. Highest chart positions: did not chart. Produced by Ian Maidman.

'Deep In Your Heart' (Brady)
Paul Brady has enjoyed a long and varied career, generally under the radar, but always highly respected by his peers. 'Deep In Your Heart' from 1985's *Back To The Centre* is a sophisticated folk/pop song, benefiting, like Roger Waters' album, from some brilliant bluesy electric guitar breaks. Brady, quoted on his website:

> I had been touring Europe with him the previous year and he liked what I was doing.

Brady returned the favour, playing on two of Clapton's solo albums: tin whistle on *Pilgrim* (1998) and guitar on *I Still Do* (2016).

Leona Boyd: ***Persona***
Recorded January 1986 at Audio International Studios, London. Released 1990. Highest chart positions: did not chart. Produced by Michael Kamen.

'Labyrinth' (Kamen)
Eric was considerably active in the session scene in the second half of the 1980s, recording with the familiar – Bob Dylan, Eric Clapton, Phil Collins, George Harrison, Jack Bruce – and the less obvious. Canadian classical guitarist Leona Boyd has been active since the early 1960s. She has won sixteen Juno awards. Her 1990 album *Persona* was produced by Michael Kamen and features Eric Clapton on the track 'Labyrinth'. This could easily be an outtake from Clapton and Kamen's soundtrack to *Edge Of Darkness*, with the same screaming guitar, pumping drum machines and synthesised strings.

Various Artists: ***Recorded Highlights Of The Prince's Trust 10th Anniversary Birthday Party***
Recorded June 1986 at Wembley Arena, London. Released April 1987. Highest position: did not chart. Produced by Andre Sheehan.

'Better Be Good To Me' (Chapman, Chinn, Knight)
'Tearing Us Apart' (Clapton, Phillinganes)

'Call Of The Wild' (Ure, Mitchell, King)
'Money For Nothing' (Knopfler, Sting)
'Everytime You Go Away' (Hall)
'Reach Out' (Armatrading)
'No One Is To Blame' (Jones)
'Sailing' (Sutherland)
'I'm Still Standing' (John, Taupin)
'I Saw Her Standing There' (Lennon, McCartney)
'Long Tall Sally' (Blackwell, Johnson, Penniman)
'Get Back' (Lennon, McCartney)

This high-profile concert was a benefit for The Prince's Trust. This would be the first of several concerts for the Trust at which Clapton would appear. Clapton is part of the house band, along with Midge Ure, Howard Jones, John Illsley, Mark King, Elton John, Mark Knopfler, and, perhaps inevitably, Phil Collins.

Guest performers include Tina Turner, Sting, Paul Young, Joan Armatrading, Rod Stewart and Paul McCartney. Clapton is 100% engaged and has a lot of fun duetting with Turner on 'Tearing Us Apart'.

Press coverage made much of Prince Charles' use of earplugs when attending this show.

Bob Dylan: *Hearts Of Fire*

Recorded August 1986 at Townhouse Studios, London. Released November 1987. Highest chart positions: did not chart. Produced by Beau Hill.

'The Usual' (Hiatt)
'Had A Dream About You' (Dylan)
'Night After Night' (Dylan)

Bob Dylan's participation in the *Hearts of Fire* film cannot be regarded as a career highlight. If you haven't seen it, then find something else to watch. Eric Clapton helped Dylan with two new songs on the accompanying soundtrack. These were recorded at The Townhouse in London in August 1986. A cover of John Hiatt's 'The Usual' has a driving riff and some resolute lead guitar, but the song is swamped by the reverbing eighties production. 'Had A Dream About You' is an unconvincing blues. Eric's solo is tight but is the kind of thing he can do in his sleep. A different mix of 'Had A Dream About You' is on Dylan's grim 1988 album *Down In The Groove*. There are three other songs known to have been recorded but were unused. 'To Fall In Love With You' is one of the great lost Dylan songs. The available recording is a one-take run through, but Dylan's vocal is exquisite. Clapton adds some tentative blues licks, embroidering the vocal perfectly. 'Some Kind Of Way (Song With No Name)', sometimes listed as 'Ride The Train', is a ragged two-chord shouter, clearly a one-take performance. Eric adds some vicious lead breaks. 'Old Five and Dimer Like Me' is a country blues written by Billie Joe Shaver, given a reggae lilt during these sessions.

Eric's contribution is not obvious. Multiple versions of many of these songs are available on bootleg.

Bob Geldof: ***Deep In The Heart Of Nowhere***

Recorded August 1986 at Bear Creek Recording Studios, Washington. Released November 1986. Highest chart positions: UK: 79, US: did not chart. Produced by Rupert Hine.

'Love Like A Rocket (album mix)' (Geldof, Stewart)
'Love Like A Rocket (7" mix)' (Geldof, Stewart)
'Love Like A Rocket (12" mix)' (Geldof, Stewart)
'Beat of the Night' (Geldof)
'August Was A Heavy Month' (Geldof)
'August Was A Heavy Month (instrumental)' (Geldof)
'Good Boys In The Wrong' (Geldof)

Boomtown Rats frontman Bob Geldof issued his debut solo album *Deep In The Heart Of Nowhere* in November 1986. Eric Clapton plays lead guitar on four tracks: these represent some of his best playing for other artists. 'Love Like A Rocket' is a commercial pop song with some unmistakable bluesy lead guitar breaks. Eric appears in the video in a fetching cardigan. 'Love Like A Rocket' was remixed for 7" release and, as was the fashion in 1986, this was also released in a longer 12" mix. The lead guitar is much more prominent here, so you need all three versions if you're collecting every EC session. Viewers of a certain age in the UK might remember Eric appearing with Geldof to mime 'Love Like A Rocket' on the BBC kids' show *Saturday Superstore* in February 1987.

'Good Boys In The Wrong' is cod-reggae with a standard EC solo which goes little to lift a tired song. 'Beat Of The Night', in contrast, is a tense semi-rap detailing a racial attack. When Geldof stops talking, Eric drops one of the best three or four solos of his career: it burns like a handful of dry ice. On 'August Was A Heavy Month', the lead guitar is practically a duet with Geldof's idiosyncratic vocals. You almost want Geldof to stop singing. Geldof told *Q* magazine at the time:

> His playing is phenomenal. I think he's played the best on this since Derek And The Dominos. I don't think even he believed how well he played. He doesn't breathe when he plays. He just closes his eyes and his touch is so sure. On one track, 'August Was A Heavy Month', I really regretted putting a vocal on because his playing was so superb.

Deep In The Heart Of Nowhere was reissued in 2005 as part of a four-disc box set called *The Great Songs of Indifference: The Anthology 1986-2001*. A different mix of 'August Was A Heavy Month' included here removes Geldof's vocal, leaving just Eric Clapton's exquisite lead guitar. As Geldof suggests, Eric's playing here is the equal of anything else in his long career.

Tina Turner: ***Break Every Rule***

Recorded September 1986 at Mayfair Studios, London. Released March 1987. Highest chart positions: UK: 2, US: 4. Produced by Graham Lyle and Terry Britten.

'What You Get Is What You See' (Britten, Lyle)
'What You Get Is What You See (single edit)' (Britten, Lyle)
'What You Get Is What You See (12" rock mix)' (Britten, Lyle)
'What You Get Is What You See (12" dance mix)' (Britten, Lyle)

Tina Turner's remarkable crossover appeal in 1984 revived a career that had seemed finished. Her album *Private Dancer* produced seven hit singles, including 'What's Love Got to Do with It', 'Better Be Good to Me', 'Private Dancer' and 'Let's Stay Together'. She and Clapton sang together on the song 'Tearing Us Apart' from his 1986 album *August* and Turner, in return, invited him to guest on her next album, *Break Every Rule*.

'What You Get Is What You See' is an up-tempo country-tinged rock track with two short, punchy solos which fight against the busy production. Released as a single in March 1987 (US: 13, UK: 30), the 7" edit is thirty seconds shorter and the 12" single includes two extraneous extended versions.

Chuck Berry: ***Hail, Hail Rock 'N' Roll***

Recorded October 1986 at The Fox Theatre, St Louis, Missouri. Released October 1987. Highest position: did not chart. Produced by Keith Richards.

'Wee Wee Hours' (Berry)
'Rock And Roll Music' (Berry)

The film *Hail! Hail! Rock 'n' Roll* celebrated Chuck Berry's sixtieth birthday. Keith Richards arranged two concerts at the Fox Theatre in St. Louis and invited a few famous friends. The soundtrack album includes Clapton singing 'Wee Wee Hours', playing a tight solo on a vintage Gibson. 'Take another one!' Berry insists. Clapton busks along on 'Rock And Roll Music', sung by Etta James.

Eric plays on a ragged version of 'School Days' as seen in the film and is also present in footage of rehearsals of several songs, including a terrific version of Berry's 'It Don't Take But a Few Minutes' where Eric picks some fabulous country guitar and a smart, spontaneous jam of 'Mean Old World'.

Robert Christgau:

> [The] film is a wickedly funny and moving rock-doc classic, exposing Berry the money-grubbing control freak, without devaluing his genius in the process.

Jon Astley: ***Everyone Loves The Pilot (Except The Crew)***

Recorded December 1986 at Revolution Studios, Manchester. Released 1987. Highest chart positions: did not chart. Produced by Phil Chapman and Andy MacPherson.

'Jane's Getting Serious' (Astley)

British record producer Jon Astley had manned the desk for *Just One Night* in 1979. He also recorded and released two albums of his own, including 1987's *Everyone Loves The Pilot (Except The Crew)*. Eric plays on 'Jane's Getting Serious', which could be a Hall and Oates outtake. The central section of 'Jane's Getting Serious' was later heard in a long-running television commercial for Heinz ketchup featuring a pre-*Friends* Matt LeBlanc, although, to these ears, it doesn't sound like the same version from Astley's album.

Jack Bruce: ***Willpower***

Jack Bruce: ***Somethin Els***

Recorded 1986-1987 at Ztudio, Zerkall, Germany. Clapton's guitar parts were recorded February 1987 in London. *Willpower* released 1989. Highest chart positions: did not chart. *Somethin Els* released 1995. Highest chart positions: did not chart. Produced by Jack Bruce, with Kurt Renker and Walter Quintus.

'Willpower' (Bruce, Brown)

'Ships In The Night' (Bruce, Brown)

'Waiting On A Word' (Bruce, Brown)

Old friend Jack Bruce benefitted from Eric's time in 1987. Bruce's 'Willpower', mostly recorded in Germany but with Eric overdubbed in London, revisits the riffs that underpinned many of Cream's songs and Eric adds a powerful, bluesy solo. 'Ships In The Night' is a 6/8 duet with Maggie Reilly which combines magnificent singing with one of Eric Clapton's best-ever solos. His delicacy of touch and perfect control is a tutorial in 'less is more'. Both songs are included on Bruce's career retrospective *Willpower*, released in 1989, on *Somethin Els* (1993) and the 6 CD box set *Shall We Follow?* (2008). *Somethin Els* also includes a third song recorded at the same sessions, 'Waiting On A Word'. This has some deftly picked fills and a quite beautiful Clapton guitar solo.

Sting: ***...Nothing Like The Sun***

Recorded March 1987 at Air Studios, Montserrat. Released October 1987. Highest chart positions: UK: 1, US: 9. Produced by Sting and Neil Dorfsman.

'They Dance Alone (Cueca Solo)' (Sting)

'Ellas Danzan Solas (Cueca Solas)' (Sting)

Sting's 'They Dance Alone (Cueca Solo)' from his second solo album *...Nothing Like The Sun* (1987), features Eric Clapton, Mark Knopfler and American jazzer

Fareed Haque on guitar. You have to listen closely to pick out Clapton's low-in-the-mix acoustic guitar playing.

The 1988 EP *... Nada Como El Sol* contains four tracks from...*Nothing Like the Sun* performed in Spanish and Portuguese. The Spanish version of 'They Dance Alone (Cueca Solo)' is 'Ellas Danzan Solas (Cueca Solas)' with translation and additional lyrics by Argentinian composer and producer Roberto Livi. The music is identical.

George Harrison: *Cloud Nine*

Recorded May 1987 at FPSHOT, Henley On Thames. Released November 1987. Highest chart positions: UK: 10, US: 8. Produced by Jeff Lynne and George Harrison.

'Cloud Nine' (Harrison)
'That's What It Takes' (Harrison, Lynne, Wright)
'Devil's Radio' (Harrison)
'Wreck Of The Hesperus' (Harrison)
Cloud Nine, the eleventh studio album by George Harrison, was recorded and released in 1987. David Wild (not my dad) described *Cloud Nine* as 'an expertly crafted, endlessly infectious record that constitutes Harrison's best album since 1970's inspired *All Things Must Pass*.' Eric plays on four songs. The title track opens with deft guitar interplay between Harrison's elegant slide guitar and Clapton's electric lead. This intensifies in a marvellous solo section. 'That's What It Takes' is a schizophrenic song. The verses are and chorus are dominated by Jeff Lynne's production, but the bridge sounds like it's been flown in from another song entirely. Keep listening for a beautifully picked guitar solo from Eric Clapton, quiet and authoritative. 'Devil's Radio' is sublime pop with another top-class solo by Eric. Finally 'Wreck Of The Hesperus' is a fine song with killer lyrics ('Ain't no more no spring chicken / Been plucked but I'm still kicking') and both Eric Clapton and Elton John doing what they do best. All-in-all, a triumph.

Various Artists: *The Princes' Trust Rock Gala*

Recorded June 1987 at Wembley Arena, London. Released 1988. Highest position: did not chart. Produced by Midge Ure.

'Running In The Family' (Gould, Badarou, King)
'If I Was' (Ure, Mitchell)
'Wonderful Tonight' (Clapton)
'Behind The Mask' (Mosdell, Sakamoto, Jackson)
'Stand By Me' (King, Leiber, Stoller)
'Through The Barricades' (Kemp)
'Saturday Night's Alright (For Fighting)' (John, Taupin)

'Reach Out, I'll Be There / I Can't Help Myself (Sugar Pie Honey Bunch) / Same Old Song' (Holland, Dozier, Holland)
'While My Guitar Gently Weeps' (Harrison)
'With a Little Help From My Friends' (Lennon, McCartney)
This time out, the house band for the annual Prince's Trust Rock Gala included Midge Ure, Mike Lindup, Mark King, Phil Collins, Mark Brzezicki and Eric Clapton. Opening with three songs from the band – Level 42's 'Running In The Family', Midge Ure's 'If I Was' and Clapton's own 'Wonderful Tonight' – a series of high-calibre singers and musicians join in turn: Tina Turner, Ben E. King, Tony Hadley and Gary Kemp, Elton John, Paul Young, George Harrison and Ringo Starr. Clapton adds his distinctive lead guitar to all of these, and is especially effective on 'Stand By Me' with Ben E. King, Spandau Ballet's 'Through The Barricades', and, thrillingly, pulling out a Gibson Les Paul for 'While My Guitar Gently Weeps' where he trades licks with ex-husband-in-law George Harrison.

Tina Turner: *Live In Europe*

Recorded June 1987 at Wembley Stadium, London. Released 1988. Highest position: UK: 8, US: 86. Produced by John Hudson.

'Tearing Us Apart' (Clapton, Phillinganes)
'Tearing Us Apart' is a track from Eric Clapton's 1986 album *August*. A duet with Tina Turner, it was released as a single in June 1987, shortly before this concert appearance at Wembley Stadium. 'Somehow, I always seem to get the best out of London,' she declares, bringing out Eric for a lively rendition of the song.

Live In Europe was released in 1988. Turner's popularity in the UK in this period ensured a top ten chart placing – impressive for a double live album.

Buckwheat Zydeco: *Taking It Home*

Recorded March 1988. Released 1988. Highest chart positions: did not chart. Produced by Rob Fraboni and Ted Fox.

'Why Does Love Got To Be So Sad' (Clapton, Whitlock)
The great American accordionist Buckwheat Zydeco first met Eric Clapton in November 1987, as described by Michael Tisserand in his illuminating book *The Kingdom Of Zydeco* (1998):

> Dural [Buckwheat Zydeco] was invited to England to play Island Records' 25th-anniversary concert. When [manager Ted] Fox and Dural arrived at the venue, they received word that they had been bumped to make room for a jam by Eric Clapton and Ringo Starr. But the manager had intended this night to be Buckwheat Zydeco's coming-out party, and he reacted quickly. Dural's

> Hammond B-3 organ was still set up, and as the rockers launched into the set, Fox grabbed the stage manager and insisted that Buck join them on stage. Recalls Fox, 'And Buck gets up there, and Clapton does this solo, and Buck played it on the organ and he bumps it up a notch. And Clapton plays what Buck has just played, and he bumps it up a notch. And they're getting into this furious cutting contest, and Clapton hasn't even turned around at this point. And all of a sudden four thousand people are screaming, and Eric just stops playing, and he puts his hand out to Buck and he says, 'I'm Eric Clapton, who are you?'

Buckwheat Zydeco toured as Clapton's support act in 1988 and 1989. Eric adds a distinctive, fiery guitar solo to his own 'Why Does Love Got To Be So Sad' released on *Taking It Home* in March 1988.

Anne Dudley: *The Robbery*

Recorded March 1988, Townhouse Studios, London. Released September 1988 on *Buster* OST. Highest chart positions: UK: 6, US: 54. Produced by Anne Dudley.

'The Robbery' (Dudley)
Clapton recorded contributions to three film and TV soundtracks in spring 1988. 'The Robbery' is an epic instrumental track recorded with composer Anne Dudley and included in the film and soundtrack to *Buster*, which starred Eric's pal Phil Collins.

Davina McCall: *unreleased sessions*

Recorded June 1988 at Townhouse Studios, London. Produced by Eric Clapton and Rob Fraboni.

Eric recorded three songs with vocalist Davina McCall in June 1988 (yes, that Davina McCall, ten years before she became a familiar face on British TV). 'I've Been Good For You', 'The Very Last Time' and 'Sticky Situation' are lightweight 80s pop with loud guitar and have never been commercially released.

Gail Anne Dorsey: *The Corporate World*

Recorded July 1988 at The Smokehouse, London. Released 1988. Highest chart positions: did not chart. Produced by Nathan East.

'Wasted Country' (Dorsey)
Gail Anne Dorsey is perhaps best known as a member of David Bowie's band for the twenty years before his death in 2016. 'Wasted Country' is the opening song from her debut solo album *The Corporate World*, produced by Clapton's regular bassist Nathan East and released in late 1988. The album is fresh and deserved more success. Clapton's solo could be straight off *Journeyman*.

Jim Capaldi: ***Some Come Running***

Recorded July 1988 at Backyard Studios, Marlow, Surrey. Released 1988. Highest chart positions: did not chart. Produced by Jim Capalidi.

'You Are The One' (Capaldi, Parren)

'Oh Lord Why Lord' (Capaldi)

Jim Capaldi is often forgotten as the 'other' singer in Traffic. His solo career was not without success, however, and he was able to recruit many famous friends for his album *Some Come Running*, recorded at his home studio in Marlow. 'You Are The One' teams Capaldi with Clapton on guitar and Steve Winwood on backing vocals. It's effortlessly funky and Eric adds a punchy solo.

'Oh Lord, Why Lord' is a more reflective song with George Harrison's slide. Eric takes two solos: the first is short but tastefully bluesy, and the second plays out the song with power and style. Eric said at the time that he performed on other songs: these remain unheard.

Carole King: ***City Streets***

Recorded December 1988 at Skyline Studios, New York. Released 1989. Highest chart positions: US: 111, UK: did not chart. Produced by Carole King and Rudy Guess.

'City Streets' (King)

'Ain't That the Way' (King)

Carole King has an impeccable pedigree. She wrote her first hit, the Shirelles' *Billboard* number one 'Will You Love Me Tomorrow' in 1959, aged seventeen. Throughout the 1960s, she co-wrote more than twenty classic songs with her husband Gerry Goffin, including 'The Loco-Motion', 'It Might as Well Rain Until September', 'Take Good Care of My Baby', 'Up on the Roof', 'I'm into Something Good', 'One Fine Day', 'Pleasant Valley Sunday' and '(You Make Me Feel Like) A Natural Woman'. Her second solo album, *Tapestry,* released in 1971, has sold over twenty-five million copies.

Unfortunately, King's 1989 album *City Streets* suffers, like so many of her peers, from sludgy 1980s production. King's singing is terrific, though. 'City Streets' has two heavily-processed and unadventurous solos from EC, who also appears in the video. 'Ain't That The Way' is much better: slower, bluesy and less obviously commercial, with Clapton's guitar accompanying King's strong vocals.

Cyndi Lauper: ***A Night To Remember***

Recorded April 1989 at The Hit Factory, New York. Released May 1989. Highest chart positions: UK: 9, US: 22. Produced by Cyndi Lauper and Lennie Petze.

'Insecurious' (Lauper, Warren, Child)

Cyndi Lauper and Eric Clapton are perhaps unlikely musical partners. How much you enjoy 'Insecurious' on Lauper's 1989 album *A Night To Remember* depends on your opinion of the shrill Brooklynite. He is double-tracked, so you get twice the Eric for your money.

Rolling Stone:

> Half of the record (particularly the cloying 'Insecurious') is somewhat disappointing.

A Night To Remember was Lauper's highest-charting album in the UK. The session date of April 1989 is recorded by Roberty: it's more likely to have been recorded during 1988 or earlier in 1989.

Zucchero Fornaciari: ***Oro Incenso E Birra***
Zucchero: ***Zucchero***
Zucchero: ***Zu & Co***

Recorded April 1989 at Power Station, New York. ***Oro Incenso E Birra*** released June 1989 (but not in the UK or the US). *Zucchero* released September 1990. Highest chart positions: did not chart. ***Zu E Co*** released May 2004. Highest chart positions: US: 84, UK: 160. Produced by Corrado Rustici. 2004 version produced by Luciano Luisi and Zucchero Fornaciari.

'Wonderful World (Italian)' (Fornaciari)
'Wonderful World (English)' (Fornaciari, Musker)
'Wonderful World (duet)' (Fornaciari, Musker)

Italian singer Zucchero Fornaciari toured as support on Eric Clapton's European tour at the beginning of 1990. Clapton had recorded a scintillating lead break in New York the previous April for the song 'Wonderful World' for Fornaciari's June 1989 album *Oro, Incenso E Birra*. At one time, *Oro, Incenso E Birra* was the all-time best-selling Italian album with over 8 million copies sold.

Fornaciari re-recorded his vocal in English for 1990's *Zucchero*, his first internationally-released album; only the lead vocal is new, the rest of the track is the same.

A third version, remixed from this 1989 recording with new vocals from Fornaciari and Clapton, is on 2004's *Zu & Co*. Clapton's guitar work is identical on all three versions, but the 2004 mix fades ten seconds later as Eric's guitar plays out the song.

Phil Collins: ***But Seriously...***

Recorded June 1989 at The Townhouse, London. Released November 1989. Highest chart positions: UK: 1, US: 1. Produced by Phil Collins and Hugh Padgham.

'I Wish It Would Rain Down' (Collins)

Phil Collins' fourth solo album, *...But Seriously*, was a huge commercial success worldwide, reaching number one in the UK, the US and another thirteen countries around the world. It was the best-selling album of 1990 in the UK and contains four top-five US singles, including 'Another Day In Paradise', 'Something Happened on the Way to Heaven', 'Do You Remember?' and 'I Wish It Would Rain Down'. This last-named was recorded during the sessions for Clapton's 'Bad Love' at the Townhouse, London, in June 1989. It's practically a duet between Collins' vocals and Clapton's lead guitar and is a top-class pop-rock song with a strong bluesy feel. The video, however, in which Clapton appears, is painful.

When released as a single in January 1990, 'I Wish It Would Rain Down' would become a major hit – number three in the US and number seven in the UK

Brendan Croker And The 5 O'clock Shadows: *Brendan Croker And The 5 O'clock Shadows*

Recorded August 1989 at Matrix Studios, London. Released 1989. Highest chart positions: did not chart. Produced by John Porter.

'This Kind Of Life' (Croker)

Brendan Croker And The 5 O'clock Shadows was Croker's fifth album and major-label debut. Producer John Porter enticed Mark Knopfler and Eric Clapton to guest on different tracks. Knopfler adds his distinctive guitar to 'No Money At All', but Clapton left his guitar at home. Apparently, he'd injured his hand in a cricket match. 'This Kind Of Life', therefore, is almost unique in Eric's guest appearances in that he sings but doesn't play.

'This Kind Of Life' is a sweet, relaxed song. Croker and Clapton harmonise brilliantly.

Producer Porter would later work with Eric Clapton on albums by Taj Mahal, John Lee Hooker, Buddy Guy and B. B. King.

The Rolling Stones: *Flashpoint*
The Rolling Stones: *Steel Wheels Live*

Recorded December 1989 at Convention Center, Atlantic City. ***Flashpoint*** released April 1991. Highest position: UK: 6, US: 16. ***Steel Wheels Live*** released September 2020. Highest position: US: 180, UK: did not chart. Produced by Chris Kimsey, Mick Jagger and Keith Richards.

'Little Red Rooster' (Dixon)
'Boogie Chillun' (Hooker)

The Rolling Stones' massive *Steel Wheels / Urban Jungle* tour was the most financially successful rock tour in history up to that point: 115 shows to six million people.

Flashpoint documents fourteen performances from the tour, recorded across the world between November 1989 and July 1990. Eric Clapton guested at the Convention Center, Atlantic City, on 19 December 1989. Eric joined the band for a slow, grinding 'Little Red Rooster' and spits a vicious guitar solo.

The album reached number six in the UK – a very strong performance for a live album.

John Lee Hooker guested on 'Boogie Chillun' at this same concert with Clapton sitting in. This is included along with 'Little Red Rooster' on the *Steel Wheels Live* album and DVD, released in 2020.

The 1990s

If Clapton's solo career in the 1990s was unfocussed – from the MOR blues-pop of *Unplugged*, through the loud blues of *From The Cradle* and the disappointing curate's egg that was *Pilgrim* – then at least he was able to play with his heroes Buddy Guy, Ray Charles, B.B. King and John Lee Hooker in this decade. There are also unlikely pairings and massive hit albums with Eternal (UK #3), Mary J. Blige (top 5 in both the US and UK) and Babyface (US #6).

Michael Kamen: ***Concerto For Saxophone & Orchestra***

Recorded March 1990 at Sarm West Studios, London. Released November 1990. Highest chart positions: did not chart. Produced by Michael Kamen and Stephen McLaughlin.

'Sandra' (Kamen)

Michael Kamen's *Concerto For Saxophone & Orchestra*, recorded in London in March 1990, follows a similar vein to his work on *Edge of Darkness* and the *Lethal Weapon* soundtracks. David Sanborn plays alto sax on several tracks, and Eric adds some bluesy guitar to 'Sandra'. The album also includes lead guitar contributions from David Gilmour and Elliot Randall.

Various Artists: ***Knebworth: The Album***

Recorded June 1990 at The Silver Clef Award Winners Concert, Knebworth House, Hertfordshire. Released August 1990. Highest position: did not chart. Produced by Chris Kimsey and Steve Smith.

'Sunshine Of Your Love' (Clapton, Bruce, Brown)
'Money For Nothing' (Knopfler)
'I Think I Love You Too Much' (Knopfler)
'Sad Songs (Say So Much)' (John, Taupin)
'Saturday Night's All Right (For Fighting)' (John, Taupin)

The Silver Clef Award Winners Concert included performances from Pink Floyd, Tears for Fears, Paul McCartney, Robert Plant and Jimmy Page, Status Quo and Genesis. And Cliff Richard. Perhaps inevitably, there was an all-star band comprising Eric Clapton, Mark Knopfler and Elton John. Five songs from this set were released on the live album in 1990. Eric, in a remarkable pink suit, plays on two Dire Straits songs and two Elton John songs, as well as his own 'Sunshine of Your Love'. Quite how many punters of the 120,000 punters wanted to hear a long tambourine solo in this show is open to question.

The 2002 DVD includes four other songs with Clapton's involvement: 'Before You Accuse Me', 'Tearin' Us Apart', 'Solid Rock' and 'Sacrifice'. 'Sunshine Of Your Love' was not included on the DVD.

Lamont Dozier: ***Inside Seduction***

Recorded December 1990 at The Hit Factory, New York. Released 1991. Highest chart positions: did not chart. Produced by Lamont Dozier and Phil Collins.

'That Ain't Me' (Dozier)

Lamont Dozier gained fame as one-third of the Holland-Dozier-Holland Motown song-writing team with brothers Brian and Eddie Holland. Between 1962 and 1967, these three men wrote ten out of the Supremes' twelve US number one singles and many great hits by the likes of Marvin Gaye, The Four Tops and The Isley Brothers.

Lamont Dozier's tenth solo album, *Inside Seduction*, was produced by Phil Collins and is a throwback to 1980s funk-pop. Dozier wrote two songs on Eric Clapton's 1986 album *August*, also produced by Collins, and the feel and mood of that album is evident here. Eric tries and fails to add some life to 'That Ain't Me'. The song 'Hold On Tight' from these sessions remains unissued.

Kate Bush: ***The Red Shoes***
Kate Bush: ***The Director's Cut***

Recorded 1990-1993 at Abbey Road Studios, London. *The Red Shoes* released November 1993. Highest chart positions: UK: 2, US: 28. *The Director's Cut* released May 2011. Highest chart positions: UK: 2, US: 186. Produced by Kate Bush.

'And So It Goes' (Bush)
'And So It Goes [Director's Cut version]' (Bush)

No one should doubt the enduring genius of Kate Bush. She was a pop star like no other: number one at nineteen with a song based on a mid-nineteenth century novel; went quietly nuts in 1982 with the eclectic album *The Dreaming*; then made one of the greatest albums of all time three years later.

Her seventh album, 1993's *The Red Shoes,* is magnificent. It was her last for twelve years. Eric Clapton plays some powerful, punchy blues riffs on 'And So Is Love', one of his best sessions for another artist. There is a remix and partially re-recorded version on the 2011 album *The Director's Cut,* which has a warmer sound with a new lead vocal. Eric's playing is retained but is pushed back into the mix a touch. This might be the superior version.

Buddy Guy: ***Damn Right I've Got The Blues***

Recorded March 1991 at Battery Studios, London. Released July 1991. Highest chart positions: UK: 43, US: 136. Produced by John Porter.

'Early In The Morning' (Hickman, Jordan, Bartley)

Buddy Guy's 1991 album *Damn Right I've Got The Blues* features Mark Knopfler, Jeff Beck and Eric Clapton. Beck and Clapton join Guy for the 6/8 jump blues 'Early In The Morning' – the three guitarists add to the audio soup, with none dominating.

Johnnie Johnson: ***Johnnie B. Bad***

Recorded March 1991 at Nomis Studios, London. Released 1991. Highest chart positions: did not chart. Produced by Terry Adams.

'Creek Mud' (Johnson, Ardolino)
'Blues #572' (Johnson)

Chuck Berry's long-time pianist Johnnie Johnson performed at Clapton's blues showcases at the Royal Albert Hall in 1990 and 1991. Eric plays on two tracks on 1991's *Johnnie B. Bad*. The slow blues 'Blues #572' has a short, tight Clapton solo. 'Creek Mud' is faster with more Eric but is decidedly pedestrian.

Richie Sambora: ***Stranger In This Town***

Recorded March 1991. Released September 1991. Highest chart positions: UK: 20, US: 36. Produced by Neil Dorfsman and Richie Sambora.

'Mr. Bluesman' (Sambora, Bryan)

Eric Clapton had met (and performed with) Bon Jovi guitarist Richie Sambora at the 1990 International Rock Awards, held at the 69th Battalion State Armory in New York. How much you enjoy 'Mr. Bluesman' from Sambora's first solo album *Stranger In This Town* depends on your definition of subtlety. Understated this ain't, but Eric's playing is terrific.

David Sanborn: ***Upfront***

Recorded November 1991 at The Power Station, New York. Released 1992. Highest chart positions: did not chart. Produced by Marcus Miller.

'Full House' (Miller, Sanborn)

Eric Clapton's working relationship dates back to 1983 when they both performed on Roger Waters' *The Pros and Cons of Hitch-Hiking* album. Of course, they may not have actually met during those sessions, but three years later, they recorded the *Lethal Weapon* soundtrack with Michael Kamen. Since then, Clapton and Sanborn have worked on the other films in the *Lethal Weapon* series and on Eric's album *Journeyman*. In 1997, they toured together as Legends with Joe Sample, Steve Gadd and Marcus Miller (who produces here).

Clapton adds delicious blues licks to the slick jazz instrumental 'Full House'.

George Harrison: ***Live In Japan***

Recorded December 1991 Tokyo Dome Stadium. Released July 1992. Highest chart positions: US, 126, UK: did not chart. Produced by George Harrison.

'I Want to Tell You' (Harrison)
'Old Brown Shoe' (Harrison)
'Taxman' (Harrison)
'Give Me Love (Give Me Peace on Earth)' (Harrison)
'If I Needed Someone' (Harrison)
'Something' (Harrison)
'What Is Life' (Harrison)
'Dark Horse' (Harrison)
'Piggies' (Harrison)
'Got My Mind Set on You' (Clark)
'Cloud 9' (Harrison)
'Here Comes the Sun' (Harrison)
'My Sweet Lord' (Harrison)
'All Those Years Ago' (Harrison)
'Cheer Down' (Harrison, Petty)
'Devil's Radio' (Harrison)
'Isn't It a Pity' (Harrison)
'While My Guitar Gently Weeps' (Harrison)
'Roll Over Beethoven' (Berry)

George Harrison's profile in 1987-1991 was as high as it had been for twenty years: 'Got My Mind Set On You' hit number one in the US and its parent album *Cloud Nine* (qv) was a resounding success. Following two well-received albums with The Travelling Wilburys, George was persuaded by his old friend Eric Clapton to perform a short tour of Japan. George's only previous solo dates, a US tour in 1974, was problematic, so Eric eased the way by offering the services of himself and his band. The setlist included many Beatles-era songs alongside selections from Harrison's solo career. It was George's final concert tour.

Eric is just one of the band here. Of course, his guitar is prominent, sharing lead duties with George and taking many solos. Especially noteworthy are the bluesy licks in 'All Those Years Ago', 'If I Needed Someone', the slow opening of 'Something' and, of course, 'While My Guitar Gently Weeps'.

Ray Charles: ***My World***

Recorded 1992. Released March 1993. Highest chart positions: US: 145, UK: did not chart.
Produced by Richard Perry.

'None Of Us Are Free' (Mann, Russell, Weil)
In theory, modernising Ray Charles' classic soul/gospel sound by incorporating elements of hip-hop and New Jack swing sounds like a good idea. In practice…

'None Of Us Are Free' is an excellent, socially-conscious song but with a busy early nineties arrangement that threatens to overwhelm. Clapton's powerful solos, strong as they are, sound flown in.

Charles' vocals are, of course, peerless. The production … well.

Solomon Burke's version, recorded with the Blind Boys of Alabama in 2002, shows just how to deliver this song.

Thomas Jefferson Kaye: ***Not Alone***

Recorded 1992. Released 1992. Highest chart positions: did not chart. Produced by Thomas Jefferson Kaye.

'Tough Enough' (Kaye)

Thomas Jefferson Kaye was an American producer, songwriter and musician who recorded two solo albums in the early 1970s.

Not Alone was his first album for nineteen years, and his last, as he died in 1994. *Not Alone* includes contributions from Steve Miller, Joe Walsh, Jeff 'Skunk' Baxter and Robby Krieger. 'Tough Enough' features Dr. John (piano), Rick Danko (bass) and Timothy B. Schmit (backing vocals), with Eric on sweet slide guitar.

Kaye was not a strong vocalist, but his albums have lots of character and are worth tracking down, especially if you're a fan of early Steely Dan: Donald Fagan and Walter Becker perform and write on Kaye's first two albums.

Clarence 'Gatemouth' Brown: ***Long Way Home***

Recorded May-September 1995 at Dockside Studios, Maurice and Sigma Sound Studios, Philadelphia, PA. Released April 1996. Highest chart positions: did not chart. Produced by Jim Bateman and John Snyder.

'Blues Power' (Clapton, Russell)

'Don't Think Twice It's All Right' (Dylan)

'Long Way Home' (Brown, Horowitz)

Clarence 'Gatemouth' Brown might not be the first name that comes to mind when you think of the classic American blues musicians, but in a long career which had already spanned fifty years in 1995 – by which time he was in his early-seventies – his spiky guitar playing influenced the likes of Albert Collins and Frank Zappa. He was also one of a small handful of blues fiddlers. Brown continued to tour extensively into his eighties and played country, jazz, Cajun music and R&B, as well as blues.

'Long Way Home' is pure acoustic blues with a typically steely solo from Eric, who was then in the middle of his *From The Cradle* blues-only tours. 'Blues Power' is a swinging cover of a song from Clapton's first solo album. It was co-written with Leon Russell, whose distinctive piano and vocals propel the arrangement. Brown and Clapton trade some terrific roadhouse blues licks.

The version of Bob Dylan's 'Don't Think Twice It's All Right', a duet with Maria Muldaur, is the exact arrangement that Clapton performed at Dylan's 30th Anniversary Concert Celebration in 1992. Clapton's playing is fluid if a touch generic.

Taj Mahal: ***Phantom Blues***

Recorded 1995. Released February 1996. Highest chart positions: did not chart. Produced by John Porter.

'Here In The Dark' (Anders)

'(You've Got To) Love Her With A Feeling' (King)

Taj Mahal is the real deal: a towering figure and brilliant musician who has never quite achieved the commercial success he deserves. Nevertheless, his respect and influence amongst his peers are significant.

Taj's version of Bernard Anders' 'Here In The Dark' is a horn-laden slow blues with massive slabs of Clapton's wailing guitar – it sounds like the harsh tones of a Gibson and is nothing short of wonderful. Paired with 'Have You Ever Loved A Woman', '(You've Got To) Love Her With A Feeling' was the b-side of Freddie King's first big hit single, released in 1960. The Taj Mahal – Eric Clapton combination offers here some pure electric blues, performed with heart and astonishing technique. Clapton's playing is quite outstanding.

Eternal: 'Someday'

Recorded 1996. Released as a single, August 1996. Highest chart positions: UK: 4, US: did not chart. Produced by Simon Climie.

'Someday' (Menken, Schwartz)

From Taj Mahal singing Freddie King to Eternal singing Disney – such is the wide range of Eric Clapton's guest sessions.

'Someday' is a song from the 1996 animated film, *The Hunchback of Notre Dame*. Released as a single in summer 1996, it became Eternal's eighth top-ten entry on the UK Singles Chart, where it peaked at number four. This is a modern R&B song with a 'Change The World' feel. Both songs were released within a few weeks of each other: Eric provides some finger-picked acoustic flourishes and a short solo to 'Someday'. The song was released in 1997 on Eternal's album *Before The Rain*, a UK number three.

For the American music market, Disney enlisted the R&B band All-4-One to sing the song. This is a different recording and Eric is not involved.

Babyface*: The Day*

Recorded 1996 in Los Angeles and New York. Released October 1996. Highest chart positions: UK: 34, US: 6. Produced by Kenneth 'Babyface' Edmonds.

'Talk To Me' (Edmonds)

Kenneth 'Babyface' Edmonds was the producer *du jour* in 1996. His work with artists such as Whitney Houston, TLC, Usher and Toni Braxton has sold many millions of records across the world.

The Day is his fourth solo album and Clapton plays some delicate electric guitar leads on the song 'Talk To Me'. Edmonds explained how the song came about, when they performed together in 1997:

> This is a song that I was working on when [Eric and I] worked together on 'Change the World'. He started playing guitar and I started smelling neck bone, grits and greens and things.

Jerry Lynn Williams: ***The Peacemaker***

Recorded 1996 at Red Bird Studios, New York. Released April 1997. Highest chart positions: did not chart. Produced by Jerry Lynn Williams.

'Sending Me Angels (Miller, Williams)
'What's This World Coming To' (Williams)
'You Better Rock Me Baby' (Williams)

Eric Clapton recorded many songs by the Texan writer, including 'Forever Man', 'See What Love Can Do', 'Something's Happening' (all on *Behind The Sun*), 'Wanna Make Love To You' (*August*-era B-side), 'Running on Faith', 'Pretending, 'Anything for Your Love', 'No Alibis' and 'Breaking Point' (all from *Journeyman*). He adds delicately picked lead guitar to three songs on Williams' 1997 solo album *The Peacemaker*. 'Sending Me Angels', co-written by Frankie Miller, who unfortunately never worked with Clapton, exposes Williams' limitations as a vocalist. His singing is drenched in reverb. We can enjoy the terrific guitar fills, though, along with two EC solos in his default style. 'What's This World Coming To' sounds like a demo, with computer drums and bass and an indifferent melody. Again, Williams' vocals are weak. The lethargic pace is lifted by Eric's beautiful guitar solo. 'You Better Rock Me Baby' is generic up-tempo rock allowing Eric to push the pace with lots of lead guitar and a great solo.

Pavarotti & Friends: ***Pavarotti & Friends (For War Child)***
Zucchero: ***Zu & Co (The Ultimate Duets Collection)***

Recorded June 1996 in Parco Novi Sad, Modena, Italy. ***Pavarotti & Friends (For War Child)*** released 1996. Highest chart positions: did not chart. Produced by Phil Ramone. ***Zu E Co*** released 2005. Highest chart positions: did not chart. Produced by Zucchero Fornaciari and Luciano Luisi.

'Run, Baby, Run' (Bottrell, Baerwald, Crow)
'Holy Mother' (Clapton, Bishop)

'Third Degree' (Boyd)
'Live Like Horses' (John, Taupin)
'Un Piccolo Auito' (Fornaciari, Salerno)
These five songs were recorded at a charity concert in Modena in June 1996. 'Run, Baby, Run', 'Holy Mother', 'Third Degree' and 'Live Like Horses' were released on *Pavarotti & Friends (For War Child)* in 1996. Eric is given performer credit on 'Holy Mother' and 'Third Degree', so they are not strictly sessions but are included here for completeness.

He adds strong, bluesy lead guitar to Sheryl Crow's performance of 'Run, Baby, Run' and also joins the ensemble finale of Elton John's 'Live Like Horses' – you can hear him adding some guitar runs over an over-blown arrangement.

In contrast, the outstanding, delicate, 'Un Piccolo Auito' pairs Clapton's supreme acoustic lead guitar with an emotional vocal by Zucchero Fornaciari. It's available on the deluxe edition of *Zu E Co* (2005). This release also includes the DVD *Zu & Co live at the Royal Albert Hall* with live versions of Zucchero's songs 'Hey Man' and 'A Wonderful World', both with Eric Clapton on lead guitar.

B. B. King: ***Deuces Wild***

Recorded 1997. Released November 1997. Highest chart positions: UK: 86, US: 73. Produced by John Porter.

'Rock Me Baby' (King, Josea)
Deuces Wild is B.B. King's thirty-fifth studio album. It was recorded with many famous musicians: Van Morrison, Tracy Chapman, Bonnie Raitt, Dr. John, Dionne Warwick, The Rolling Stones, Joe Cocker, David Gilmour, Willie Nelson and others. Mick Hucknall also performs.

Eric plays and sings on a new version of King's 1964 hit single 'Rock Me Baby'. They work well together, in an irresistible combination that would flower on *Riding With The King*, recorded three years later.

Bill Wyman's Rhythm Kings: ***Struttin' Our Stuff***

Recorded 1997 at TV-Studio Ohne Filter, Baden-Baden, Germany. Released February 1998. Highest chart positions: did not chart. Produced by Bill Wyman and Terry Taylor.

'Melody' (Jagger, Richards, Preston)
The first studio album from Bill Wyman's Rhythm Kings includes this version of The Rolling Stones' 'Melody', first recorded for *Black And Blue* (1976), where it is credited to 'Jagger/Richards, inspiration by Billy Preston'.

Not known as a singer ('(Si Si) Je Suis un Rock Star', anyone?), Wyman hands vocal duties to Georgie Fame and Beverley Skeete. Eric busks along and drops a tight, trebly solo.

Babyface: ***MTV Unplugged NYC 1997***

Released September 1997 at Hammerstein Ballroom, New York. Released November 1997. Highest chart positions: US: 106, UK: did not chart. Produced by Alex Coletti.

'Change the World' (Sims, Kennedy, Kirkpatrick)

'Talk to Me' (Edmonds)

Eric guests at Babyface's MTV showcase. They perform the two songs they had recorded together the previous year. Eric sings and plays on 'Change The World, ' changing the acoustic arrangement into harder, faster electric version. This really rocks. 'Talk To Me' has a funky backbeat to which Eric effortlessly adds his best blues licks.

Original Soundtrack: ***Blues Brothers 2000***

Recorded 1997 in Toronto. Released February 1998. Highest chart positions: did not chart. Produced by Paul Schaffer.

'How Blue Can You Get?' (Feather)

'New Orleans' (Guida, Royster)

I tried to pretend that this doesn't exist.

Blues Brothers 2000 is a limp follow-up to the 1980 comedy film *Blues Brothers*. It ends with a Battle Of The Bands between the Blues Brothers Band and the so-called Louisiana Gator Boys, a top-heavy one-off collaboration that wastes the talents of Eric Clapton, B. B. King, Jeff 'Skunk' Baxter, Gary US Bonds, Clarence Clemons, Bo Diddley, Isaac Hayes, Dr. John, Charlie Musselwhite, Billy Preston, Lou Rawls, Koko Taylor, Travis Tritt, Jimmie Vaughan, Grover Washington Jr., and Steve Winwood. They each get half a line of lead vocals and/or a few bars of instrumental soloing and about five seconds of screen time.

The songs performed, both included on the soundtrack album, are King's 'How Blue Can You Get' and Bonds' 'New Orleans'. For completists only.

The Jimmy Rogers All-Stars: ***Blues Blues Blues***

Recorded 1997. Released 1999. Highest chart positions: did not chart. Produced by John Koenig.

'That's All Right' (Rogers)

'Blues All Day Long' (Rogers)

'Boom Boom' (Hooker)

Another series of a-list collaborators – this time including Jeff Healey, Jagger and Richards, Taj Mahal, and Stephen Stills – join blues guitarist Jimmy Rogers for modern re-recordings of some of his best-known songs. Rogers, not to be confused with the Singing Brakeman country crooner or the American pop singer both called Jimmie Rogers, was the guitarist in Muddy Waters' band in the 1950s. He was a huge influence on the likes of Jimmy Page and Eric Clapton, both of whom contribute to a loose version of John Lee Hooker's 'Boom Boom', listed on the album as 'Gonna Shoot You Right Down'. This track started out as a jam between Rogers and Clapton. Page's guitar and Robert Plant's vocals were added later. Other than some blasting blues harmonica, no one really distinguishes themselves.

'Blues All Day Long' provides contrast between Rogers' deep growling vocals and Clapton's tenor. Eric's solo is perfect: short, bright, focussed, tight. Clapton's best performance, though, comes on 'That's All Right', a Rogers original from 1950. With a wonderful live feel, the band gets into a solid slow blues groove, with a great vocal from Rogers, tinkling piano from Johnnie Johnson, Carey Bell providing fine harmonica accompaniment in the Little Walter tradition and Eric on strong vocals and a stellar guitar solo.

Blues, Blues, Blues was Rogers' last album: he died between recording and release.

John Lee Hooker: *The Best Of Friends*

Recorded 1998 (probably). Released October 1998. Highest chart positions: did not chart. Produced by John Porter and Mike Kappus.

'Boogie Chillun' (Hooker)

John Lee Hooker's series of collaborative albums from 1989 to 1997 showcased the charisma of this blues legend, mixing new songs with re-recordings of older material.

The compilation album *The Best Of Friends* highlights choice performances from these albums. Hooker duets and/or plays guitar with the likes of Van Morrison, Bonnie Raitt, Carlos Santana, Ike Turner, Ry Cooder, Jimmie Vaughan and Los Lobos. There are two new songs. Eric plays on a re-recording of 'Boogie Chillun', first recorded in 1948. His playing is hard and loud.

Bill Wyman's Rhythm Kings: *Anyway The Wind Blows*

Recorded 1998. Released December 1998. Highest chart positions: did not chart. Produced by Bill Wyman and Terry Taylor.

'Gee Baby, Ain't I Good To You' (Razaf, Redman)

This time various Rhythm Kings include Peter Frampton, Gary Brooker, Albert Lee, Paul Carrack and Chris Rea.

'Gee Baby, Ain't I Good To You' is a jazz standard first recorded in 1929. It's been performed by hundreds of artists since, perhaps most notably by Nat 'King' Cole (1944) and Ray Charles (1967), both of whom inform this recording which has bristling lead guitar from Eric Clapton and a rich lead vocal from Georgie Fame.

Mary J. Blige: ***Mary***

Recorded 1998-1999. Released August 1999 (US), October 1999 (UK). Highest chart positions: UK: 5, US: 2. Produced by Manuel Seal and Nate-Love Clemons.

'Give Me You (Album Mix)' (Warren, Blige)

Mary J. Blige's fourth album showed a more mature side of the New York-born singer. 'Give Me You', in its original album version, is a torch ballad, uplifting and strong despite Diane Warren's trademark trucker's modulation.

There is no guitar solo as such, but some thick Ernie Isley riffs underpin the chorus. The album was a big hit in both the UK and US.

'Give Me You' was released as a single in March 2000 in a new dance mix. Eric is not obviously audible on this, nor on any of the five other remixes released across two CD singles.

Françoise Hardy: ***Clair-Obscur***

Recorded 1998. Released May 2000. Highest chart positions: did not chart. Produced by Michel Bernholc.

'Contre Vents et Marées' (Clapton, Hardy)

Whilst not technically a session, Françoise Hardy uses, I believe, the original recording of Clapton's 'Theme From A Movie That Never Happened' as the basis for her song 'Contre Vents et Marées' released in 2000 on *Clair-Obscur* and as the theme tune to the French TV soap *Cap Les Pins (Tide of Life)*.

Clapton is not credited on this album; the guitarist listed is Hardy's fifteen-year old-son, Thomas Dutronc, as this translation from *Françoise Hardy, Un Long Chant D'amour* by Frédéric Quinonero in 2017 shows:

> Approached by the producer of *Cap des Pins*, a new French TV series for France 2, Françoise Hardy has the mission of finding a song for the opening/closing credits. She proposes an Eric Clapton acoustic instrumental, created for a film which never aired and on which she was considering overlaying vocals. The song, recorded at Plus XXX with Thomas Dutronc on the guitar, is called 'Contre Vents et Marees' and is then included on the *Clair-obscur* album.

That's the official story. But close listening, with both tracks loaded to multi-track software and played simultaneously, leaves no doubt in my mind that the backing track is Clapton's original instrumental. The guitar phrasing is identical and Clapton's playing is unmistakable. Listen for yourself.

Tony Rich Project: ***Birdseye***

Recorded 1998. Released August 1998. Highest chart positions: UK: did not chart. Produced by Tony Rich.

'Silly Man' (T. Rich)
'No Time Soon' (T. Rich)
'Thoughts of Leavin'' (DuBose, J. Rich)
'My Stomach Hurts' (T. Rich)
The Tony Rich Project mixes acoustic, folk-flavoured pop with modern soul. Think of Stevie Wonder and Marvin Gaye distilled through D'Angelo and Babyface with a nineties production.

Rich has a smooth, soulful voice. He plays every instrument on these songs other than Clapton's guitar solos.

'Silly Man' is not so far from Clapton's work on *Pilgrim*. Eric adds a few subtle Stratocaster licks but does not take a solo. He is more prominent on 'No Time Soon': his delicately picked electric guitar practically duets with Rich. Clapton adds a short solo to the dreary 'Thoughts of Leavin'' but shines with a trademark flurry of notes on 'My Stomach Hurts'.

Clapton is credited as simply 'E'.

The Band: *Jubilation*

Recorded spring 1998. Released September 1998. Highest chart positions: did not chart. Produced by Aaron Hurwitz and The Band.

'Last Train to Memphis' (Danko, Helm, Hudson, Ciarlante, Weider, Bell, Charles)
If there were questions asked when The Band reformed without Robbie Robertson in 1983, then the suicide of Richard Manuel in 1986 should have been the end, the very last waltz.

But, against the odds, the remaining trio established a stable line-up and recorded three excellent albums: *Jericho* (1993), *High On The Hog* (1996) and *Jubilation* (1998). Whist not comparable to their original run of albums between 1968 and 1976 – what is? – these three records by The Band are warm, fun, professional and full of highlights.

Eric Clapton adds a rockabilly solo to the down-home original song 'Last Train to Memphis', which sounds like the soundtrack to the best party in town.

Producer Aaron Hurwitz, at theband.hiof.no:

> Bobby Charles, who wrote 'See You Later, Alligator' and 'Walkin' To New Orleans,' used to live in Woodstock and hung around with The Band. He sent 'Last Train to Memphis' to Levon, who added some verses and gave it a real party feel. It's as much about Beale Street and the Cotton Festival as it is about Elvis.

Rick Danko (interviewed by Paul James for CBS Radio):

> [Eric] was very busy at this time. Called him up and asked him. We ended up sending a tape to England, he put the guitar part on, and sent it back. I liked it.

> We made this record for ourselves; it was made for the art of the music. It had nothing to do with taking the money and running.

Danko died in 1999; Helm in 2012.

Various Artists: ***A Very Special Christmas Live***
Recorded December 1998 in Washington D. C. Released October 1999. Highest chart positions: did not chart. Produced by Bobby Shriver.

'Christmas Blues' (Hite, de la Parra, Wilson, Taylor, Vestine)
'Christmas Tears' (Wilson, Thompson)
'Give Me One Reason' (Chapman)
'Merry Christmas Baby' (Baxter, Moore)
'Santa Claus Is Coming To Town' (Coots, Gillespie)
A Very Special Christmas Live is the fourth of twelve specially-recorded compilation albums released between 1987 and 2013, which have raised over $100 million. These performances were recorded at an event in Washington D. C. on 1 December 1998.

John Popper, vocalist and harmonica player in Blues Traveler, sings 'Christmas Blues'. Eric Clapton, very dapper in suit and tie, adds some trademark blues guitar. Clapton sings Freddie King's 'Christmas Tears', which is the highlight of the set. His singing and playing is very good indeed, especially the final solo where he spits out note after note of blues. Clapton would re-record this song for his 2018 album *Happy Xmas*. He duets with Tracy Chapman on her big hit 'Give Me One Reason', an unexpected pairing that works surprisingly well, smooth and vibrant. 'Merry Christmas Baby' pairs Sheryl Crow and Eric Clapton: Crow sings beautifully and Eric plays some funky blues rhythm guitar on two tight if unremarkable solos.

The closing 'Santa Claus Is Coming To Town' is the ensemble finale performed by an uneasy mix of Mary J. Blige, Jon Bon Jovi, Tracy Chapman, Eric Clapton, Sheryl Crow, John Popper, Run-D.M.C. and Vanessa Williams. Clapton sings one line and jams a little with Popper. The Clintons beam benevolently.

Santana: ***Supernatural***
Recorded 1999 at Fantasy Studios, Berkeley, California. Released June 1999. Highest chart positions: UK: 1, US: 1. Produced by Carlos Santana.

'The Calling' (Santana, Thompson)
'The Calling Jam' (Santana, Thompson)
Supernatural is Santana's eighteenth studio album and has sold over thirty million copies. A few years earlier, the Latin rock band didn't have a record deal. This radio-friendly album includes the massive hit single 'Smooth', a US

number one. Guest artists include Eric Clapton, Rob Thomas, Eagle-Eye Cherry, Lauryn Hill, Dave Matthews, Maná, KC Porter and CeeLo Green.

Clapton plays on 'The Calling'. He had reconnected with Carlos Santana in February 1999 at the Grammy Awards ceremony in Los Angeles. Santana had supported Clapton on his 1975 US tour, and they had both appeared as guests at a Bob Dylan concert in London in 1984.

'The Calling', eight minutes in length, starts as a slow, moody guitar duet. The pace picks up and the two men exchange powerful guitar phrases to a vocal refrain of 'hear me calling'. 'The Calling' would win the award for Best Rock Instrumental Performance at the 42nd Annual Grammy Awards. A 'Legacy Edition' of *Supernatural* was released in February 2010, with a second disc including 'The Calling Jam', a remix and edit of the first four minutes of 'The Calling'.

Jack Bruce: *Shadows in the Air*

Recorded November 1999-December 2000. Released July 2001. Highest chart positions: did not chart. Produced by Jack Bruce and Kip Hanrahan.

'Sunshine Of Your Love' (Clapton, Bruce, Brown)
'White Room' (Bruce, Brown)
Jack Bruce's objectives are not quite clear here, as he re-records two of his Cream classics with Latin rhythms and loads of percussion. Eric gamely joins in, but the only word I can use is 'horrible'.

Sheryl Crow: *Live From Central Park*

Recorded September 1999 at East Meadow, Central Park, New York. Released December 1999. Highest chart positions: US: 107, UK: did not chart. Produced by Sheryl Crow.

'White Room' (Bruce, Brown)
'Tombstone Blues' (Dylan)
Eric rocked up to play lead guitar on two tracks at Sheryl Crow's concert at New York's Central Park on 14 September 1999. The Dixie Chicks, Stevie Nicks, Chrissie Hynde, Keith Richards and Sarah McLachlan also contribute on various tracks.

Eric generously revisits an old Cream classic, 'White Room' singing the verses and going full wah on the solo. Crow sings the bridge. It's a decent version, with kudos to Jim Bogios, the long-time drummer of Counting Crows, who keeps the song moving at a fair clip. 'Tombstone Blues' is an all-hands-on-deck finale. Eric adds a short solo.

2000 onwards

Clapton's session work has continued in the last twenty-plus years. Whilst less frequent than in previous decades, he has found time to work with old friends Paul, Ringo, J. J. Cale and Brian Wilson and added astounding, career-high guitar to albums by Joe Cocker, the Rolling Stones, Robbie Robertson, Sonny Landreth and the Allman Brothers Band.

He can still surprise us as well: Eric Clapton is surely the only musician to have recorded and performed live with both Hawkwind and Ed Sheeran.

Jamie Oldaker: *Mad Dogs And Okies*

Recorded July 2001-2005. Released August 2005. Highest chart positions: did not chart. Produced by Jamie Oldaker.

'Wait Til Your Daddy Gets Home' (Gill, DiPiero)
'Positively' (Ramsey)
Jamie Oldaker was the drummer in Eric Clapton's band from 1974 to 1979 and again in 1984-1985. Oldaker, in his press release for the album:

> It all started in 2001 when I decided to record a bunch of songs written by Oklahoma natives. Of course, the project originally came from a selfish standpoint because that's where I'm from and that's where I got started, working with Leon Russell at his Shelter Records and branching off from there. I wanted to get a bunch of my friends together and make an album like we used to years ago – go into the studio, perform the songs live, and forget the ProTools.

Mad Dogs and Okies is an unexpected joy and a good-time atmosphere infuses all fifteen songs, recorded with the likes of Vince Gill, Peter Frampton, Taj Mahal, Willie Nelson, J. J. Cale, Bonnie Bramlett and Marcy Levy.

Gill and Clapton trade juicy licks on Gill's 'Wait Til Your Daddy Gets Home', which could be a J. J. Cale outtake or a remake of 'Long Tall Sally'. Clapton sings Willis Alan Ramsey's 'Positively', a lovely laid-back country/gospel tune with Clapton on Dobro (credited to Ramsay, but it sounds like Clapton's style).

Jools Holland His Rhythm & Blues Orchestra And Friends: *Small World Big Band*

Recorded 2001 at Helicon Mountain Recording Studios, London. Released November 2001. Highest chart positions: UK: 8, US: did not chart. Produced by Laurie Latham.

'What Would I Do Without You' (Charles)
Jools Holland's series of '...And Friends' albums pairs his Rhythm & Blues Orchestra with A-list guests. *Small World Big Band* (2001) has a spinetingling cover of Ray Charles' 'What Would I Do Without You'.

Eric has recorded many songs by Ray Charles over the years. Here his newly emergent strength as a singer is put to the test: he passes, brilliantly. There's also a slow-burning guitar solo with every note chosen carefully.

In some territories, this album was released under the name *Jools Holland's Big Band Rhythm & Blues.*

Paul McCartney: ***Driving Rain***

Recorded October 2001 at Madison Square Garden, New York and Quad Studios, New York. Released November 2001. Highest chart positions: UK: 46, UK: 26. Produced by David Kahne.

'Freedom' (McCartney)

Paul McCartney's 'Freedom' was written in response to the 11 September attacks in 2001. This was performed at the Concert For New York City on 20 October 2001 with Eric on lead guitar. The song was rush-released as a single a week later, with a new lead vocal from Paul, and is also on McCartney's *Driving Rain* album. The original live version is on *The Concert For New York*, released in 2002.

Brian Wilson: ***Gettin' In Over My Head***

Recorded 2002–04 at Bear Creek Recording Studios, Washington. Released June 2004. Highest chart positions: UK: 53, US: 100. Produced by Brian Wilson.

'City Blues' (Wilson, Bennett)

Gettin' In Over My Head is the fourth solo studio album by American musician Brian Wilson, the creative genius, of course, behind The Beach Boys. Wilson was enjoying a critical and commercial renaissance, mostly due to well-received recent live performances of his legendary 1960s albums *Pet Sounds* and *Smile*.

Alexis Petridis, in *The Guardian* on 11 June 2004:

> Wilson's previous solo efforts contained moments when he appeared to rediscover the inspiration that fuelled the Beach Boys' peerless mid-1960s recordings: his eponymous 1988 album had 'Love and Mercy', 1996's *Imagination* offered the lovely 'Lay Down Burden'. You wait in vain for something similar here. Everyone wants Brian Wilson's story to have a happy ending. The worst thing about *Gettin' In Over My Head* – far worse than the mediocre songs and the MOR guest appearances – is that it doesn't sound terribly happy.

'City Blues' allows Eric to add some loud but generic lead guitar. Wilson adds buckets of reverb.

Ringo Starr: ***Ringo Rama***

Recorded 2002 at Starr's recording studio in London. Released March 2003.

Highest chart positions: US: 113, UK: did not chart. Produced by Mark Hudson and Ringo Starr.

'Never Without You' (Starkey, Hudson, Nicholson)
It's wholly appropriate that Eric contributed to Ringo Starr's moving tribute to George Harrison with 'Never Without You' from Ringo's actually-quite-good 2002 album *Ringo Rama*. Eric's solo is edgy and liquid, and he adds much to this excellent track.

The Crusaders: ***Rural Renewal***
Recorded 2002 in Los Angeles. Released March 2003. Highest chart positions: did not chart. Produced by Stewart Levine.

'Rural Renewal' (Sample)
'Creepin'' (Sample)
The Crusaders released *Rural Renewal* in 2003, their first album for twenty years. Crusaders' main man Joe Sample had performed with Clapton in the Legends band in 1997 and had joined Clapton's band on the guitarist's Far East Tour in 1997, as well as sessions for *Pilgrim* (1998), *Riding With The King* (2000) and *Reptile* (2001).

Clapton plays on 'Rural Renewal' and 'Creepin'', two perfect jazz-funk instrumentals. Eric's playing sits in the pocket; his playing is not flashy but is an integral element of this impeccable music. 'Rural Renewal' has a deft electric guitar solo, and 'Creepin'' winds an acoustic guitar melody around the horns and Joe Sample's electric piano. Delightful.

Wynton Marsalis Septet: ***United We Swing***
Recorded June 2003 at the Apollo Theater, New York. Released March 2018. Highest chart positions: did not chart. Produced by Ashley Schiff Ramos.

'I'm Not Rough' (Armstrong, Armstrong)
In June 2003, Eric joined the Wynton Marsalis Septet for one of the jazz trumpeter's annual series of concerts to benefit the Jazz at Lincoln Center programme. This version of Louis Armstrong's 'I'm Not Rough' features Eric on sprightly acoustic and vocals with a jazz septet of trumpet, saxophone, clarinet, trombone, piano, bass and drums. It's quite unlike anything else with which Clapton has been involved.

Marsalis and Clapton later performed a full concert together, recorded and released as *Play the Blues: Live from Jazz at Lincoln Center* in 2011.

Buddy Guy: ***Blues Singer***
Recorded 2003 at Sweet Tea, Oxford, Mississippi. Released June 2003. Highest chart positions: did not chart. Produced by Dennis Herring.

'Crawlin' Kingsnake' (Hooker, Bosman)
'Lucy Mae Blues' (Sims)
'I Love the Life I Live' (Dixon)
Eric once again worked with Buddy Guy in 2003: the all-acoustic *Blues Singer* is about as authentic as you can get. The version here of John Lee Hooker's 'Crawling King Snake' is transcendent, with both Clapton and B. B. King adding their unmistakable guitar styles to this superb track. Clapton also trades tingling guitar licks with Guy on the gently swinging 'Lucy Mae Blues' and the tense 'I Live the Life I Love'. One wishes for a full album of this irresistible combination.

J. J. Cale: *Roll On*

Recorded 2003-2009 at 'Britannia Studio' (this from the album sleeve notes, precise location unknown). Released February 2009. Highest chart positions: did not chart. Produced by J. J. Cale.

'Roll On' (Cale)
JJ Cale's fourteenth and final studio album released in his lifetime ploughs a familiar furrow and is very much an extension of *The Road To Escondido*.

Eric plays on the title track, which is a typical Cale shuffle. It has a neat rockabilly guitar solo.

Jools Holland His Rhythm & Blues Orchestra: *Jack O' The Green*

Recorded 2003 at Helicon Mountain Recording Studios, London. Released November 2003. Highest chart positions: UK: 39, US: did not chart. Produced by Laurie Latham.

'Message To My Son' (Clapton, Holland, Burke)
'Mabel' (Clapton, Holland, Burke)
Jack O' The Green pairs Clapton with Solomon Burke on two original compositions: 'Message To My Son' and 'Mabel'. These are up-tempo, soulful and fun. Eric's playing is relaxed: he's one of the band here, and his solos comment rather than dominate.

Although he doesn't appear on the album, Clapton worked again with Burke in 2008, writing the title track of *Like A Fire*. This song has a very Clapton feel, brooding and soulful with an attractive acoustic guitar solo (Dean Parks shines, here) and some 'Signe'-like chord changes. Burke sings brilliantly. Clapton and Burke also co-wrote the shuffling, upbeat and light-of-touch 'Thank You' from the same album. *Like A Fire* was produced by Clapton's some-time bandmate Steve Jordan and it's a shame that Eric doesn't play on these songs.

Toots and The Maytals: *True Love*

Recorded 2003-2004. Released April 2004. Highest chart positions: did not chart. Produced by Richard Feldman.

'Pressure Drop' (Hibbert)

'Take A Trip' (Hibbert, Livingstone)

Toots and The Maytals were one of the best-known Jamaican reggae bands, active from 1962 until 2020. *True Love* is a collection of their classics re-recorded with guest artists including Willie Nelson, Eric Clapton, Jeff Beck, Trey Anastasio, No Doubt, Ben Harper, Bonnie Raitt, Manu Chao, The Roots, Ryan Adams, Keith Richards, and The Skatalites.

Eric appears on two tracks. His squalling wah-wah guitar is all over the remake of the Maytals' most celebrated song, the infectious 'Pressure Drop'. 'Take A Trip' features vocals by Toots and Bunny Wailer, one of the original Wailers trio. Again, Eric adds burning guitar licks and is given lots of space to shine.

Toots Hibbert died in 2020, Bunny Wailer in 2021.

The Crickets: ***The Crickets and their Buddies***

Recorded 2003-2004. Released July 2004. Highest chart positions: did not chart. Produced by Greg Ladanyl.

'Someone, Someone' (Greines, Petty)

Eric first worked with The Crickets in 1970 (qv). Eric joins them once more on an album to re-record some of their famous and lesser-known tracks. Rodney Crowell, Phil Everly, J.D. Souther, Johnny Rivers, Nancy Griffith, Albert Lee, Bobby Vee and Waylon Jennings also contribute.

Eric adds smooth guitar lines and a sincere vocal to a track first released in 1959 as the B-side to the single 'Love's Made a Fool of You'.

Willie Nelson: ***Live and Kickin'***

Recorded April 2003 at the Beacon Theatre, New York. Released June 2003. Highest chart positions: US: 42, UK: did not chart. Produced by James Stroud.

'Night Life' (Breeland, Buskirk, Nelson)

'Night Life' was recorded at the Beacon Theatre in New York on 9 April 2003 to celebrate country legend Willie Nelson's seventieth birthday. Nelson gathered together a remarkable cast of peers and friends for a TV special. Ordered alphabetically: Ray Charles, Kenny Chesney, Elvis Costello, Sheryl Crow, Wyclef Jean, Norah Jones, Toby Keith, Diana Krall, Lyle Lovett, Shelby Lynne, John Mellencamp, Ray Price, Paul Simon, Shania Twain, Steven Tyler and Z.Z. Top. Luckily the music overcomes the extreme schmaltz of the occasion.

A healthy and relaxed Clapton sings and plays with great affection, making his skill and charisma seem utterly effortless. He doesn't stick around for the ensemble run through the obligatory 'On The Road Again', though.

Various Artists: ***The Concert For George***

Recorded 29 November 2002 at the Royal Albert Hall, London. Released November 2003. Highest chart positions: US: 97, did not chart. Produced by Jeff Lynne.

'Arpan' (Shankar)
'I Want to Tell You' (Harrison)
'If I Needed Someone' (Harrison)
'Old Brown Shoe' (Harrison)
'Give Me Love (Give Me Peace on Earth)' (Harrison)
'Beware of Darkness' (Harrison)
'Isn't It a Pity' (Harrison)
'Photograph' (Harrison, Starkey)
'Honey Don't' (Perkins)
'For You Blue' (Harrison)
'Something' (Harrison)
'All Things Must Pass' (Harrison)
'While My Guitar Gently Weeps' (Harrison)
'My Sweet Lord' (Harrison)
'Wah-Wah' (Harrison)
'Horse To The Water' (Harrison)

The resonant and poignant *Concert For George* is wonderful from start to finish. Go out and buy it now!

George Harrison died on 29 November 2001, aged 58. His memorial concert was held at the Royal Albert Hall in London on the first anniversary of his death. It was organised by Harrison's widow and son, Olivia and Dhani, under the musical direction of Eric Clapton. The profits from the event went to the Material World Charitable Foundation, an organisation founded by Harrison.

The pedigree of the musical selections and contributors is without peer.

The show opened with a set of Indian classical music written by George's great friend Ravi Shankar and performed by a large ensemble of Indian musicians led by Anoushka Shankar. Eric Clapton adds his distinctive acoustic to the lengthy piece 'Arpan', a style of music with which Eric has no precedence. The Monty Python troupe do some silly things. The house band for the 'rock' section comprised Clapton with Jeff Lynne (guitar), Marc Mann (guitar), Andy Fairweather Low (guitar), Dhani Harrison (guitar), Gary Brooker (keyboards), Chris Stainton (keyboards), Billy Preston (keyboards), Dave Bronze (bass), Henry Spinetti (drums), Jim Keltner (drums), Ray Cooper (percussion), Jim Horn (saxophone), Tom Scott (saxophone), Katie Kissoon (backing vocals), Tessa Niles (backing vocals) and Sam Brown (backing vocals). Many of these had their moment in the spotlight and various guests came and went. Jeff Lynne opened with a solid 'I Want to Tell You', Clapton takes the lead on a brilliant 'If I Needed Someone' followed by Gary Brooker's fine rendition of 'Old Brown Shoe' and Lynne's 'Give Me Love (Give Me Peace on Earth)'. Eric sings 'Beware of Darkness' before short sets by Joe Brown (two songs), Sam Brown (a show-stopping 'Horse To The Water') and Tom Petty and the Heartbreakers (three songs). The house band return to perform a sublime 'Isn't It a Pity', with vocals by Clapton and Billy Preston before introducing

Ringo Starr to sing 'Photograph' and 'Honey Don't'. Starr sits at the drums for the rest of the set. Paul McCartney sings an unexpected 'For You Blue', and joins Clapton for a duet of 'Something'. A transcendent 'All Things Must Pass', sung by McCartney (a song rejected by The Beatles in 1969; Klaus Voormann is on bass here) is followed by a marvellous version of 'While My Guitar Gently Weeps', sung by Clapton, who is given a chance to stretch out on guitar. Dhani Harrison goes up to Clapton at the end of the performance and thanks him. 'My Sweet Lord', sung by Preston, and an ensemble 'Wah-Wah' are a suitable double-whammy finale. Although everyone stays on stage for the encore of 'I'll See You In My Dreams', only Joe Brown's band actually perform this emotional tribute to a fine musician.

The album contains all of these performances with the exception of 'Horse To The Water', which can be seen as part of the entire concert on the DVD release, on which Jeff Lynne remarks:

> [It] was a fantastic way of letting it all go, of letting George go, even though he was surely watching. I'm sure he was happy that his good pals were there for him. Sometimes, I'd look around, wondering, 'Where's George?' He was the only thing missing.

Bruce Hornsby: *Halcyon Days*

Recorded 2004 at Olympic Studios, Barnes. Released August 2004. Highest chart positions: US: 86, UK: did not chart. Produced by Wayne Pooley and Bruce Hornsby.

'Gonna Be Some Changes Made' (Hornsby)
'Halcyon Days' (Hornsby)
'Candy Mountain Run' (Hornsby)

Halcyon Days is the eighth studio album by American singer and pianist Bruce Hornsby, who has scored success with his band The Range in the 1980s and as a latter-day member of the Grateful Dead. His solo career contains many intriguing albums which are difficult to classify but easy to enjoy. 'Gonna Be Some Changes Made' opens with off-kilter percussion and piano, scat vocals and a catchy chorus. It's four minutes before Clapton jumps out of the arrangement with a trademark solo. Eric sings harmony vocals as well as playing two powerful guitar solos on the dynamic 'Candy Mountain Run'. The lethargic but atmospheric 'Halcyon Days' is a Sting / Hornsby duet. Clapton adds a short, delicate, gorgeous solo. It's one of his best for other artists.

Clapton's parts were recorded remotely with Simon Climie at Olympic: the rest of the album would be laid down at Hornsby's home studio, Tossington Sound, in Williamsburg, VA.

Hubert Sumlin: *About Them Shoes*

Recorded 2004. Released 2005. Highest chart positions: did not chart. Produced by Rob Fraboni.

'I'm Ready' (Dixon)

'Long Distance Call' (Morganfield)

Hubert Sumlin was Howlin' Wolf's guitarist from 1954 until 1976, Wolf's death. As such, he participated in *The London Howlin' Wolf Sessions* (qv), recorded with Eric Clapton in May 1970.

More than thirty years later, Clapton contributes to Sumlin's *About Them Shoes,* a refreshing blues album comprising of songs by Muddy Waters and Willie Dixon. Dixon's 'I'm Ready' opens the album. Eric Clapton is on lead guitar and vocals and The Band's Levon Helm sits on the drum stool. 'Hubert!', Clapton shouts ahead of some tasty lead guitar. Some gritty harmonica from Paul Oscher (a member of Muddy Waters' band for several years) leads to Clapton's own, typically fluid guitar solo. Eric also sings and plays on a loose but tough version of Waters' 'Long Distance Call'.

Keith Richards also performs on this excellent album.

Joe Cocker: *Heart and Soul*

Recorded 2004. Released October 2004. Highest chart positions: UK: 61, US: did not chart. Produced by C. J. Vanston.

'I Put A Spell On You' (Hawkins)

One might question the logic behind a remake of Screamin' Jay Hawkins' 'I Put A Spell On You', which is familiar in versions by artists as diverse as Nina Simone, Alan Price, Creedence Clearwater Revival and Bryan Ferry.

In practice, though, the final result is spine-tingling: the quiet arrangement and Cocker's matter-of-fact delivery turns the song from a sexual boast to a gentle threat. Clapton's solo is outstanding.

Les Paul: *Les Paul & Friends: American Made World Played*

Recorded 2004. Released August 2005. Highest chart positions: did not chart. Produced by Bob Cutarella, Fran Cathcart and Simon Climie.

'Somebody Ease My Troublin' Mind' (Cooke)

The studio pioneer Les Paul was almost ninety when he recorded this mixed bag with an overabundance of guests. Many notable singers and guitarists contribute: Joss Stone, Sting, Steve Lukather, Kenny Wayne Shepherd, Edgar Winter, Peter Frampton, Billy Gibbons, Neal Schon, Beth Hart, Jeff Beck, Keith Richards, Rick Derringer, Buddy Guy, John Rzeznik, Steve Miller and Joe Perry. Mick Hucknall also performs.

Eric singing Sam Cooke's 'Somebody Ease My Troublin' Mind' sounds on paper like a good idea. To re-use Cooke's disembodied vocals from 1964, however, simply smacks of sensationism. Cooke was one of the greatest singers of all time, so despite a lovely solo from Eric, the listener is uneasy about the principles behind this attempt at resurrection. Les Paul, the artist's name on the cover, let's not forget, is all but inaudible.

Marcus Miller: ***Silver Rain***
Recorded 2004 at Bear Creek Recording Studios, Washington. Released March 2005. Highest chart positions: did not chart. Produced by Marcus Miller

'Silver Rain' (Miller, Clapton Kibble, Withers)
Clapton's Legends bandleader Marcus Miller, formerly of Miles Davis' band and hundreds of sessions, invited Eric to sing and play on the title track to the 2005 album *Silver Rain*.

This smooth funk/reggae crossover suits Clapton like a Versace whistle. His singing, sometimes overlooked due to his prowess on the guitar, is wonderful. We have short, tight bass, trumpet and saxophone solos ahead of a dynamic play out from Clapton.

Rod Stewart: ***Stardust – The Great American Songbook Vol 3***
Recorded 2004. Released October 2004. Highest chart positions: US: 1, UK: 3. Produced by Steve Tyrell and Clive Davis.

'Blue Moon' (Rodgers, Hart)
Since his first solo album in 1969, Rod Stewart has shown an uncanny knack for reworking other people's songs. But the series of *Great American Songbook* albums released between 2002 and 2010 dilutes Stewart's talents to crooning.

I cannot think why anyone would want to listen to this more than once, other than to enjoy Eric Clapton's sharp acoustic guitar solo.

Jerry Lee Lewis: ***Last Man Standing***
Recorded December 2004-May 2006 at Phillips Studio and Sun Studio in Memphis, Tennessee and 'various other studios'. Released September 2006. Highest chart positions: US: 26, UK: did not chart. Produced by Steve Bing and Jimmy Ripp.

'Trouble In Mind' (Jones)
Another big-name collaboration album which illustrates the respect afforded to, and influence made on, well-known musicians such Jimmy Page, B. B. King, Bruce Springsteen, Mick Jagger, Keith Richards, Ron Wood, Neil Young, Robbie Robertson, John Fogerty, Ringo Starr, Merle Haggard, Rod Stewart, George Jones, Willie Nelson, Buddy Guy, Don Henley and Kris Kristofferson, all of whom appear here. One can only imagine what Paul McCartney thinks of Jerry Lee Lewis and Little Richard belting out 'I Saw Her Standing There'.

Jerry Lee sings 'Trouble In Mind', written by jazz pianist Richard M. Jones in 1924 and recorded by Dinah Washington and Nina Simone. It's a close cousin of 'Key To The Highway'. Clapton's solo is mixed high and loud with plenty of distortion.

B. B. King & Friends: ***80***
Recorded 2005 in the USA and the UK. Released September 2005. Highest chart positions: US: 45, UK: did not chart. Produced by John Porter.

'The Thrill is Gone' (Hawkins, Darnell)
80 pairs B. B. King with an impressive line-up of A-listers. They each rework a B.B. King standard, with a pretty good hit rate, although one questions whether this album adds anything at all to King's original versions. Clapton adds a light touch to 'The Thrill Is Gone', one of King's signature songs first recorded in June 1969 for *Completely Well* and performed at just about every King concert for the next forty-five years. King will have sung 'The Thrill Is Gone' thousands of times and this version is pleasant but hardly thrilling.

Hiroshi Fujiwari: ***Cappuccino***
Recorded 2004. Released in Japan only, January 2006. Highest chart positions: did not chart. Produced by Hiroshi Fujiwara.

'Cappuccino' (Clapton, Fujiwara, Matsutoya)
'Cappuccino Lite (Samba de froresta Remix)' (Clapton, Fujiwara, Matsutoya)
'MIME (K.U.D.O Remix)' (Clapton, Fujiwara)
'MIME' (Clapton, Fujiwara)
This release straddles the fence between a session and a collaboration. Clapton co-wrote 'Cappuccino' and 'MIME' and is jointly credited on the EP which has been released only in Japan.

'Cappuccino' is a cool jazz song; Eric plays acoustic lead. The vocals by veteran singer Yumi Matsutoya are in Japanese. Matsutoya has sold around 40 million albums in Japan since 1968. The 'Samba de froresta Remix' adds flutes, cello and forest sound effects. The dryer production brings Eric's playing much closer.

'MIME' has tasteful electric guitar over bubbling electro-jazz. The remix by Masayuki Kudo (aka DJ K.U.D.O.) has a sunny dub reggae feel. Beautiful.

Sam Moore: ***Overnight Sensational***
Recorded 2006. Released August 2006. Highest chart positions: did not chart. Produced by Randy Jackson.

'You Are So Beautiful' (Preston, Fisher)
Eric contributes to the next in a long line of collaborative albums, this time for half of the soul duo Sam and Dave, who had hits with 'Soul Man', 'Hold On, I'm Comin'', 'You Don't Know Like I Know', 'I Thank You', 'When Something is Wrong with My Baby' and many others. *Overnight Sensational* pairs Moore with a mixed bag of guests including Jon Bon Jovi, Bekka Bramlett, Mariah Carey, Billy Gibbons, Vince Gill, Paul Rodgers, Bruce Springsteen, Sting, Travis Tritt, Steve Winwood and Wynonna Judd.

'You Are So Beautiful' is a Billy Preston song first released in 1974. Joe Cocker's version was a huge hit in early 1975. This version pairs Moore and

Preston with Italian singer Zucchero. Preston also plays piano; Eric Clapton adds delicate lead guitar. The song was nominated for the award for Best Traditional R&B Vocal Performance at the 49th Grammys.

This is believed to include Billy Preston's final studio performances. He died on 6 June 2006.

Tony Joe White: ***Uncovered***

Recorded 2006. Released September 2006. Highest chart positions: did not chart. Produced by Jody White and Tony Joe White.

'Did Somebody Make A Fool Out of You?' (White)

Tony Joe White is perhaps best known as the writer of 'Polk Salad Annie' and 'Rainy Night in Georgia' at the end of the 1960s and, much later, 'Steamy Windows' for Tina Turner.

His relaxed 2006 album *Uncovered* features collaborations with Mark Knopfler, Michael McDonald, J.J. Cale and Eric Clapton. Clapton's wide-open guitar solo and warm vocals on 'Did Somebody Make A Fool Out of You?', a new version of a song first released in 1973, were recorded remotely in London and added to the album via digital technology. You wouldn't know.

Robert Randolph & The Family Band: ***Colorblind***

Recorded 2006. Released October 2006. Highest chart positions: did not chart. Produced by Pete Kipley.

'Jesus Is Just Alright' (Reynolds)

Robert Randolph has been listed as one of *Rolling Stone*'s 100 greatest guitarists of all time. With his Family Band (including brother Marcus on drums and sister Lenesha on vocals), he mixes soulful funk of acts such as Earth, Wind and Fire and Sly and the Family Stone with eviscerating pedal steel guitar. The Family Band toured as Clapton's support act in 2004 and 2008. Randolph would regularly join Clapton for an encore of 'Got My Mojo Working'.

Readers of a certain age will recognise 'Jesus Is Just Alright' from versions by The Byrds (1969) and The Doobie Brothers (1972). This version easily tops both of these: Randolph and band push Clapton hard and plays brilliantly. He also sings a verse.

Pinetop Perkins: ***Pinetop Perkins And Friends***

Recorded 2007-2008. Released June 2008. Highest chart positions: did not chart. Produced by Doug Nelson.

'How Long Blues' / 'Come Back Baby' (Carr/Davis)

Joe Willie 'Pinetop' Perkins, born in 1913, worked as pianist with blues greats Robert Nighthawk, Earl Hooker Sonny Boy Williamson, John Lee Hooker, Howlin' Wolf and Muddy Waters. He recorded his signature song 'Pinetop's

Boogie Woogie' in 1953 at Sam Phillips's Sun Studio in Memphis, Tennessee: the song was already thirty years old at this stage, but Perkins' version became so well known that he took his nickname from it. To celebrate his 95th birthday, he recorded an album with the likes of B. B. King and Jimmie Vaughan. Clapton plays on 'How Long Blues' / 'Come Back Baby', a duet between Perkins and with his Indiana neighbour, blues singer Nora Jean Brusco.

Producer Doug Nelson, in the album's press release:

> Nobody's ever put those two songs together before. I asked Pine if he thought it would work and if it would be right to do it. He liked the idea, and it ended up sounding like magic. We're both very proud of that track. Everyone who came to this project came to it with their hearts wide open, and they all brought their best to the table. I've worked on some great projects, but until I worked on this record with Pine, I'd never had the opportunity to work on a project that came together with such a palpable sense of love and respect.

Clapton's playing is clean and understated, never taking the focus from Perkins' laid back, warm vocals.

Sonny Landreth: *From The Reach*

Recorded 2007. Released May 2008. Highest chart positions: did not chart. Produced by Sonny Landreth and Tony Daigle.

'When I Still Had You' (Landreth)
'Storm of Worry' (Landreth)

Sonny Landreth's career has been unduly ignored for far too long. Predominantly a slide guitarist, he has spent time in John Hiatt's and Jimmy Buffett's bands as well as enjoying a long parallel solo career. 2007's *From The Reach* is his eleventh solo album. It features appearances by Buffett, Robben Ford, Vince Gill, Dr. John and Mark Knopfler, amongst others. Landreth, in the album's sleeve notes:

> It's the classic dream come true. I wrote these songs with these guests in mind as a tribute to their influence on me. Inviting them to come aboard led us down some amazing paths.

Eric Clapton plays on two songs. Landreth and Clapton face off on the hard rocking 'When I Still Had You' with each guitarist panned hard right and left in the stereo spectrum. Clapton's playing is loud and fierce and he adds some strong backing vocals for good measure. 'Storm of Worry' is a slow blues and again, Eric plays superbly, punctuating Landreth's vocals lines with fierce stabs of guitar. His solo is overdriven, forceful and furious. Terrific stuff.

Steve Winwood: ***Nine Lives***

Recorded 2007-2008 at Wincraft Studios, Gloucestershire. Released April 2008. Highest chart positions: US: 12, UK: did not chart. Produced by Steve Winwood.

'Dirty City' (Winwood, Godwin)

Old friends Steve Winwood and Eric Clapton toured together to great acclaim in late winter and spring 2008. Winwood's *Nine Lives* album was released shortly afterwards and Clapton adds some loud, dirty guitar to the eight-minute 'Dirty City', which revisits the slinky funk-rock crossover of early Traffic.

Their joint album *Live from Madison Square Garden* is out of the scope of this book, but it's wholeheartedly recommended. Eric cuts loose on old Traffic and Blind Faith tracks as well as gems from his solo back catalogue. Best of all, he delivers outstanding versions of Jimi Hendrix' 'Voodoo Chile' and Buddy Miles' 'Them Changes'.

David Sanborn: ***Here And Gone***

Recorded 2008. Released June 2008. Highest chart positions: did not chart. Produced by Phil Ramone.

'I'm Gonna Move to the Outskirts of Town' (Weldon, Jordan)

Resuming his long-term working relationship with jazz saxophonist David Sanborn, Eric sings Ray Charles in a track that could have sat nicely on his *Clapton* or *Old Sock* albums. Sanborn honks away, the horn section is impeccable and Clapton plays some very clean lead guitar lines.

Dr. John and the Lower 911: ***City That Care Forgot***

Recorded 2008 in Maurice, LA. Released June 2008. Highest chart positions: did not chart. Produced by Mac Rebennack and Herman Roscoe Ernest.

'Time For A Change' (Rebennack, Charles)
'Stripped Away' (Rebennack, Rose)
'City That Care Forgot' (Rebennack)

The City That Care Forgot is Dr. John's twenty-seventh album of greasy Voodoo N'Awlins funk. The compact 'Time For A Change' features Eric riffing freely over bluesy changes and the whomp of parping horns. It's utterly irresistible. 'Stripped Away is seriously funky with some sharp, decisive licks from Clapton, who is high in the mix and takes the song to a tight conclusion. The brooding, mysterious title track has Ani DiFranco on backing vocals and guitar and EC playing excellent and very prominent distorted blues guitar lines.

Buddy Guy: ***Skin Deep***

Recorded 2008 at Blackbird Studios, Nashville. Released July 2008. Highest chart positions: US: 68, UK: did not chart. Produced by Tom Hambridge.

'Every Time I Sing The Blues' (Hambridge, Nicholson)
Eric sings and plays on another album by his friend and mentor, Buddy Guy. 'Every Time I Sing The Blues' is a powerful song written by producer Tom Hambridge. It's based on regular blues changes but with a lop-sided arrangement and wide-open spaces in the rhythm. Both men sing and play superbly, absolutely in sync with each other – Clapton has some real grit in his throat and stretches out with some dynamic soloing. He ends with a sneaky musical quote from 'All Your Love' dating back to his John Mayall days.

Robbie Robertson: ***How To Become Clairvoyant***
Recorded 2008-2011 at The Village Recorder, Los Angeles; Olympic Studios, London. Released April 2011. Highest chart positions: US: 13. UK: did not chart. Produced by Marius de Vries and Robbie Robertson.

'He Don't Live Here No More' (Robertson)
'The Right Mistake' (Robertson)
'This Is Where I Get Off' (Robertson)
'Fear of Falling' (Clapton, Robertson)
'She's Not Mine' (Robertson)
'Madame X' (Clapton)
'Won't Be Back' (Clapton, Robertson)
'Fear Of Falling (demo)' (Clapton, Robertson)
'Madame X (demo)' (Clapton)
'He Don't Live Here No More (demo)' (Robertson)
'The Right Mistake (demo)' (Robertson)
'Won't Be Back (demo)' (Clapton, Robertson)
'She's Not Mine (alternative mix)' (Robertson)
David Fricke in *Rolling Stone* on 4 April 2011:

> It is fitting that Eric Clapton, who once aspired to join The Band, sings and plays on half of this record. His and Robertson's grizzled vocals and pointillist guitar exchanges in 'The Right Mistake' and 'Fear of Falling' (the latter with throaty bolts of organ by Steve Winwood) are sublime roughage, the sound of two men with shared roots still moving forward.

It took Robbie Robertson eleven years between disbanding The Band and releasing his first solo album. And another thirteen between his fourth solo album, 1998's *Contact from the Underworld of Redboy* and *How to Become Clairvoyant*. Clapton plays on seven tracks, sings on one, co-writes two and – unusually – donates a song.

Robertson to *Huffington Post* in 2011:

> The beginning of this record really started with Eric and I just messing around with some ideas. We didn't really have anything that specific in mind, except

> that we're old friends and we've been talking about doing something for a while. So, he was in L.A. some years ago, we were playing around with ideas and talking about life, and those stories ended up in the music and the songs — that was the germ of the idea. Then, Eric had to go off to a tour of Japan at the time, and I had a film project, so we just went off and sort of forgot about what we had done. Then, sometime after that, I stumbled over this music again, not realizing how much of this music we had started. I called him and said, 'You know, I just revisited this stuff, and some of it is further along than I thought, and some of it is really good.' His reply was, 'I know that.' (laughs) Just because it was a passing thing, I didn't realize how far in we had gotten on this. Then he said, 'Listen, why don't we work out some of these ideas and see what happens? Come and do it in London, and we'll do it with [bassist] Pino [Palladino], [drummer] Ian [Thomas], you and I, and then if we need a keyboard player, we'll see if Steve Winwood is around, and maybe he'll help us too.'

Palladino and Thomas comprised Clapton's rhythm section in mid-2008, which might suggest a timeline for these recordings.

'He Don't Live Here No More' is a powerful rock song ladled with slabs of Eric's electric guitar and slide. There are also two flamenco-style acoustic guitar breaks which are performed by Robbie Robertson. 'The Right Mistake' has unmistakably fluid, luscious Clapton solos and Steve Winwood on organ.

The atmospheric 'This Is Where I Get Off' has a warm production, a dark Robertson vocal and some delicately picked blues licks from Clapton. Delicious trade-off soloing from Clapton and Robinson lifts the song markedly. 'Fear of Falling' is a very commercial song that enters 'Change The World' territory with nylon-strung acoustic guitars, buzzing Hammond and an exceptional Clapton lead vocal. Robertson adds his own distinctive electric guitar flourishes and sings in the bridge. This section does not appear in the demo, suggesting this is Robertson's compositional contribution. Clapton brings out his Strat towards the end. Lovely.

'She's Not Mine' harks back to the widescreen ambient Daniel Lanois production of Robertson's 1987 debut album. Eric plays a supporting role without dominating. The central guitar solo is heavily manipulated. In contrast 'Madame X' is an instrumental solely written by Clapton, who takes a prominent role on gut-string guitar. Robinson plays the electric guitar here. It's utterly gorgeous.

Finally, 'Won't Be Back' is a Clapton / Robertson co-composition. The music feels 100% Eric, and his guitar dominates. Robertson plays shimmering electric guitar and sings lead, Clapton harmonises. It's like these two old friends are sitting on rocking chairs on a back porch.

The album was released in a deluxe edition containing five bonus tracks: four demos and the exclusive track 'Houdini'. Eric is most audible on his own 'Fear

Of Falling' – on which Robertson does not sing, unlike the final version – and the instrumental 'Madame X'. It sounds like his acoustic solo on the demo of 'He Don't Live Here No More' and he might also play the shimmering electric guitar on 'The Right Mistake' (equally, that could be Robertson's playing but as the part is replicated on the final version, and it's Clapton there, so it could be him here too). I don't believe that Eric performs on either the demo version of 'This Is Where I Get Off' or on 'Houdini'.

The skeletal demo of 'Won't Be Back', for which Eric wrote the music and on which he plays acoustic guitar, is available only on the Japanese edition of *How To Become Clairvoyant* and also as part of a limited edition collectors' set which includes a triple vinyl LP, a double CD and a DVD. The latter includes an alternative mix of 'She's Not Mine'.

Paul Jones: ***Starting All Over Again***

Recorded 2008. Released March 2009. Highest chart positions: did not chart. Produced by Carla Olson.

'Choose Or Cop Out' (Jones)
'Starting All Over Again' (Mitchell)

Paul Jones was the singer in Manfred Mann from 1962 to 1966, following up his time in this band with a move into musical theatre and a long-running, high-profile blues programme on BBC Radio 2 from 1986 to 2018. Jones had sung with The Powerhouse with Eric Clapton in 1966, and has been the frontman of The Blues Band since 1979. *Starting All Over Again* was his first solo album for thirty-seven years. Eric Clapton generously sprinkles blues riffs over the indifferent and rather mannered songs 'Choose Out Or Cop Out' and 'Starting All Over Again'.

Jeff Beck: ***Performing This Week – Live At Ronnie Scott's Deluxe Edition***

Recorded 10 November 2008 at Ronnie Scott's Jazz Club, London. Released 2015. Highest chart positions: did not chart. Produced by Alan Branch.

'Little Brown Bird' (Morganfield)
'You Need Love' (Dixon)

Jeff Beck's live album *Performing This Week* was recorded in late 2008 and released the following year. It showcases Beck as a rare talent. As if you didn't know. The original release does not include Clapton's performances of Muddy Waters' 'Little Brown Bird' and Willie Dixon's 'You Need Love': you need the 2015 deluxe edition. Clapton takes the lead vocals on both songs and despite some stellar playing from EC, it's Beck that shines brightly here.

Allman Brothers Band: ***Beacon Box Set 2009***

Recorded 19 and 20 March 2009 at the Beacon Theater, New York. Released 2009. Highest chart positions: did not chart. Produced by The Allman Brothers Band.

19 March 2009
'Key To The Highway' (Broonzy, Segar)
'Dreams' (Allman)
'Why Does Love Got To Be So Sad' (Clapton, Whitlock)
'Little Wing' (Hendrix)
'Anyday' (Clapton, Whitlock)
'Layla' (Clapton, Gordon)

20 March 2009
'Key To The Highway' (Broonzy, Segar)
'Stormy Monday' (Walker)
'Dreams' (Allman)
'Why Does Love Got To Be So Sad' (Clapton, Whitlock)
'Little Wing' (Hendrix)
'In Memory Of Elizabeth Reed' (Betts)
'Layla' (Clapton, Gordon)

Eric Clapton joined the Allman Brothers Band for two shows during their regular annual residency at the Beacon Theater in New York. These were his first-ever public performances with the Allmans. These shows were released as part of an immense forty-seven CD box set which documents all fifteen 2009 shows in their entirety.

Apart from Eric, there are guest appearances from Taj Mahal, Levon Helm, Larry Campbell and Teresa Williams, Johnny Winter, Cesar Rojas and David Hidalgo, Buddy Guy, Trey Anastasio and Page McConnell, Boz Scaggs, Robert Randolph, Randy Brecker, Stanley Clarke, John Hammond, Bonnie Bramlett, Susan Tedeschi, Scott Boyer and Tommy Talton (of Cowboy), Sheryl Crow, Southside Johnny, Bruce Hornsby, Bernard Purdie, John Bell, Jimmy Herring, Bob Margolin, Sonny Landreth, Billy Gibbons, Kid Rock, Ivan Neville, Berry Oakley Jr and Devon Allman, Chuck Leavell, Phil Lesh and Bob Weir: an impressive roster in anyone's book.

Clapton joined for the second set of each show, performing five songs from his Derek and the Dominos period – 'Key To The Highway', 'Why Does Love Got To Be So Sad', 'Little Wing', 'Anyday' and 'Layla' – as well as sitting in for the Allman Brothers' classics 'Stormy Monday', 'Dreams' and 'In Memory Of Elizabeth Reed'. The musicianship is impeccable.

Derek Trucks, reflected to *Rolling Stone* on the fifteen-minute version of 'In Memory of Elizabeth Reed':

> That was a different side of him that I hadn't seen. Where he normally would have gotten to his point, stayed and got out, he got in, stayed and realized he wasn't nearly finished. He kept ploughing. There was a freedom and unhinged element to it that I really dug.

Joe Bonamassa: *Live from the Royal Albert Hall*

Recorded May 2009 at The Royal Albert Hall, London. Released October 2009. Highest chart positions: did not chart. Produced by Kevin Shirley.

'Further on Up the Road' (Robey, Veasey)

There's no doubting Joe Bonamassa's pedigree and skill as a blues guitarist and singer. His delivery, though, can be curiously sterile.

Eric joined him on-stage in London on 4 May 2009 to reprise 'Further On Up The Road', Clapton's preferred encore number for many years. Bonamassa and Clapton share lead vocals and play alternating solos, the type of which they can both play in their sleep. It doesn't even approach the incendiary versions on *1934-1976*, *The Last Waltz* and *Secret Policeman's Other Ball – The Music* detailed elsewhere in this book. The static, well-heeled London audience can't have helped.

This performance was released on the album and DVD *Live from the Royal Albert Hall*.

Bruce Hornsby and The Noisemakers: *Levitate*

Recorded 2009. Released September 2009. Highest chart positions: US: 116, UK: did not chart. Produced by Bruce Hornsby and Tony Berg.

'Space Is The Place' (Emory, Collier, Hornsby)

Bruce Hornsby's furious 'Space Is The Place' from 2009's *Levitate* has some energising but way-back-in-the-mix lead guitar.

Clapton joined Hornsby for a rare US television performance on *The Tonight Show* in September 2009. Drummer and co-writer of 'Space Is The Place' Sonny Emory joined Clapton's band in 2018 and spoke to artsatl.org that year:

> Fast forward to when Jay Leno took over *The Tonight Show*. Bruce Hornsby was the musical guest, and Eric came and sat in with us. We actually played a song I wrote called, 'Space is the Place.' One day I got a call from Eric, and he told me he kept remembering what it felt like to play with me on Jay Leno and that he wanted me to come play drums for him. That was an intense moment to absorb. I remember thinking to myself that I had some tremendous shoes to fill.

Paul McCartney: *Kisses On The Bottom*

Recorded 2010-2011 in London, Los Angeles and New York. Released February 2012. Highest chart positions: US: 5, UK: 2. Produced by Tommy LiPuma.

'My Valentine' (McCartney)
'Get Yourself Another Fool' (Henry, Tucker)

In his prime, Paul McCartney was equally adept at singing, songwriting and bass playing. Perhaps prompted by Rod Stewart's series of *Great American*

Songbook albums (2002-2010), McCartney's 2012 album *Kisses On The Bottom* consists primarily of covers of traditional pop music and jazz arranged by Diana Krall. McCartney writes only two of the fourteen tracks. He plays the bass on none of them. Thankfully, McCartney's voice had yet to fall victim to sixty-plus years of smoking, drinking, long concert tours and, well, old age. Clapton's acoustic leads on 'My Valentine' are subtle and appropriate and his tight, fluid electric playing on 'Get Yourself Another Fool' is magnificent.

As a thank-you, Macca duetted on a cheesy version of 'All Of Me' with Clapton on the latter's *Old Sock* (2013).

Chris Barber: *Memories Of My Trip*

Recorded in 2010. Released in 2011. Highest chart positions: did not chart.

'Weeping Willow' (Fuller)

Chris Barber was one of the UK's jazz scene's most enduring and important figures, primarily through his own Chris Barber Band from 1954. Lonnie Donegan, who played with Barber at the time, was given his first break by Barber in 1954. Donegan influenced many of the key British players of the sixties – John Lennon was singing a Donegan song the day he met Paul McCartney – and Barber himself arranged the first UK tours of blues artists such as Big Bill Broonzy, Sonny Terry and Brownie McGhee, and Muddy Waters. This sparked young musicians such as Peter Green, the Rolling Stones and Eric Clapton.

Memories Of My Trip celebrates Barber's eightieth birthday and contains material from many of his bands over the years, with guest spots by Van Morrison, Paul Jones and Mark Knopfler. Blind Boy Fuller's 'Weeping Willow', first recorded in 1937, has Eric on vocals and tasty Dobro. It's wonderous.

John Fordham in *The Guardian* on 2 June 2011:

> Celebrating visionary British trad-jazz veteran Chris Barber's 80th, this two-disc set includes encounters with Van Morrison, Mark Knopfler, Dr. John and Eric Clapton, among others – testaments to how influential Barber was for a generation of rockers enthused not only by his dedication to jazz's roots, but also by an unsectarian attitude some purists saw as heretical. Van Morrison's account of trad icon Ken Colyer's 'Goin' Home' is a showcase for him and for long-time Barber trumpeter Pat Halcox, and a magnificently clamorous 1976 version of 'Oh Didn't He Ramble' with Van Morrison and Dr. John is one of the standouts – as is the band's tight riffing under the nimble lines of New Orleans clarinettist Albert Nicholas on 'C. Jam Blues'. A ruminative 'Blues Stay Away From Me' features Mark Knopfler on guitar and vocals and a rough cassette-captured jam between the wah-wah-blasting Barber on trombone and R'n'B hero Muddy Waters is an unexpected treasure.

Barber, one of the most important post-war British musicians, died aged 90 on 2 March 2021.

Jerry Douglas: *Traveler*

Recorded 2011 in Nashville, New Orleans, New York and Banbury. Released June 2012. Highest chart positions: did not chart. Produced by Russ Titelman.

'Something You Got' (Kenner)

Lap-steel and Dobro maestro Jerry Douglas has appeared on over 1,600 albums as a session player and has produced dozens of albums by the likes of Alison Krauss and the Del McCoury Band. Primarily known in the country music field, Douglas is equally adept at almost any kind of music. He has played with the top jazz, pop, and country artists for fifty years, releasing sixteen solo albums and garnering fourteen Grammys along the way.

'Something You Got' is an unexpected diversion into soulful R & B, previously covered by artists as diverse as Wilson Pickett, Fats Domino, Bobby Womack, The Moody Blues, the Searchers, Fairport Convention and Bruce Springsteen.

Clapton sings a duet here. The first guitar solo is pure Jerry Douglas, the second classic Clapton – slow, easy, magnificent.

Paul Wassif: *Looking Up Feeling Down*

Recorded 2011. Released September 2011. Highest chart positions: did not chart. Produced by Paul Wassif and David Watson.

'Please Don't Leave' (Wassif)
'Southbound Train' (Broonzy)

Paul Wassif is a British guitarist who had been a member of the band Distant Cousins, the support act on Clapton's 1998 tour. Wassif stayed friendly with Clapton and subsequently worked with legendary folkie Bert Jansch, as he told *Where's Eric* in 2011:

> I had been playing with Bert for a while and Eric had come along to see us play at Somerset House [April 2007]. A few days later, I was having supper with Eric and he basically told me that I needed to get out there and start doing my own stuff. A few days later, while I was still contemplating Eric's comments, Bert effectively told me the same thing. Even for me, this was difficult to ignore!

Wasiff's first solo album, *Looking Up Feeling Down*, was released in September 2011 and achieves the feat of the UK's premier post-war blues and folk guitarists playing together. 'Southbound Train' sets Clapton into the familiar territory of a steady, possibly over-long Big Bill Broonzy blues – Eric pulls out his Dobro for some scintillating playing. As a singer, Wassif is a great guitarist. His own 'Please Don't Leave' is a gentle acoustic minor seventh ballad that misses a trick as neither Jansch nor Clapton takes a solo. Their strumming could be anyone.

Sonny Emory: *Rock Hard Cachet*

Recorded 2012 in the Atlanta and London. Released March 2013. Highest chart positions: did not chart. Produced by Sonny Emory.

'Truth'll Set U Free' (Borden, Kennedy, Keck)

Drummer Sonny Emory was a member of Earth, Wind & Fire between 1987 and 1999 has been part of Bruce Hornsby's band since 2002. As a session player, he performed on the soundtrack of the 1989 feature film *Lethal Weapon 2* with Eric Clapton. Emory in conversation with artsatl.com:

> I originally met Eric in 1986 when I was working with David Sanborn. David brought me in to work on the *Lethal Weapon 2* soundtrack, and Eric was working on it, too. I was really gassed to be on the same project with him. Then he came to see me when I was playing with Earth, Wind & Fire and told me afterwards that he enjoyed my playing — which was a huge honour. That led to my calling him on a whim and to ask him to play on my album, *Rock Hard Cachet*, while recording it in Europe. When he said he'd do it, I was floored.

'Truth'll Set You Free' is a funky tune, little more than a riff with excellent lead vocals by Atlanta-based soul singer Kipper Jones. Clapton grinds some distorted guitar leads

Johnny Winter: *Step Back*

Recorded 2013-2014. Released September 2014. Highest chart positions: US: 17, UK: did not chart. Produced by Paul Nelson.

'Don't Want No Woman' (Robey)

Johnny Winter found his niche in 1968 and stuck to it.

Step Back is his nineteenth album of guitar-based blues-rock featuring performances of familiar songs by Ray Charles, Willie Dixon, Howlin' Wolf, Bo Diddley, Clarence 'Gatemouth' Brown, Jimmy Reed, B.B. King, Son House, Little Richard, Lightnin' Hopkins and Fats Domino. Guest musicians include Jason Ricci, Dr. John, Billy Gibbons, Joe Perry, Leslie West and Brian Setzer. Do we really need new versions of 'Killing Floor', 'Long Tall Sally' and 'Who Do You Love?'

The cover of Don Robey's 'Don't Want No Woman' features Winter and Clapton trading guitar licks – in truth, Clapton doesn't sound wholly engaged and Winter takes the garlands here.

Winter died on 16 July 2014, after the album was finished but before release. *Step Back* won the Grammy Award for Best Blues Album category in 2015.

Nathan East: ***Nathan East***

Recorded 2013 at British Grove Studios, London (probably). Released March 2014. Highest chart positions: did not chart. Produced by Chris Gero, Marcel East and Nathan East.

'Can't Find My Way Home' (Winwood)

Nathan East has appeared on more than 2,000 albums over the past 35 years. He has toured as part of Eric Clapton's band most years since 1986. *Nathan East* is his debut solo album and this classy version of Blind Faith's 'Can't Find My Way Home' is sumptuously produced. Clapton is all over it.

East has sung the song many times as part of Clapton's band since 1989.

Kurt Rosenwinkel: ***Caipa***

Recorded c. 2013. Released February 2017. Highest chart positions: did not chart. Produced by Kurt Rosenwinkel.

'Little Dream (Rosenwinkel)

The Rolling Stones, Ed Sheeran, Kurt Rosenwinkel, Hawkwind: evidence that Eric Clapton knows no musical boundaries. American guitarist Rosenwinkel had met Clapton in 2012 and appeared at the 2013 Crossroads Guitar Festival. 'Little Dream' is a flowing jazz song with strong Brazilian influence and subtly picked electric guitar – Eric sits in the background and embellishes rather than dominates.

The Rolling Stones: ***Blue And Lonesome***

Recorded in December 2015 at British Grove Studios, London. Released December 2016. Highest chart positions: UK: 1, US: 4. Produced by Don Was, Mick Jagger and Keith Richards.

'I Can't Quit You Baby' (Dixon)

'Everybody Knows About My Good Thing' (Grayson, Horton)

Eric Clapton reconfirmed his long-term friendship with The Rolling Stones in 2015. *Blue and Lonesome* was recorded in just three days at Mark Knopfler's British Grove Studios in London. Clapton was contemporaneously recording *I Still Do* at the same studio.

Eric adds some super slide guitar to 'Everybody Knows About My Good Thing', originally recorded by Little Johnny Taylor in 1971. Clapton, Richards and Wood mesh together brilliantly here, as they do on Willie Dixon's 'I Can't Quit You Baby' (first recorded by Otis Rush in 1956). 'Yeah, go, Eric,' an over-excited Jagger shouts. And go he does – magnificently.

Blue And Lonesome was a big success: number one in the UK and number four in the US. The band was awarded the Grammy Award for Best Traditional Blues Album in 2018, their first Grammy in 23 years.

Ed Sheeran: ***Divide***

Recorded 2016. Released March 2017. Highest chart positions: UK: 1, US: 1. Produced by Benny Blanco.

'Dive' (Sheeran, Levin, Michaels)

Sheeran was the first global YouTube superstar, and this is a payback of sorts. Eric is credited on Ed Sheeran's *Divide* as Angelo Mysterioso, a pseudonym used by George Harrison on Cream's *Goodbye* (recorded 22 years before Sheeran was born!) and by Sheeran himself on Clapton's song 'I Will Be There' from 2016's *I Still Do.*

Clapton's solo sounds like's it's being played in the bathroom down the hall.

Divide sold 232,000 physical and digital copies in the UK on its first day of release and debuted at number one on the US *Billboard* 200. 'Dive' was released as a single, reaching number eight in the UK and 49 in the US.

Hawkwind: ***Road To Utopia***

Recorded 2018. Released September 2018. Highest chart positions: did not chart. Produced by Dave Brock and Mike Batt.

'The Watcher' (Kilminster)

For their thirty-first album, Hawkwind re-recorded highlights from their back catalogue, improbably arranged and produced by Mike Batt, the man behind 'Bright Eyes', Katie Melua and the musical exploits of The Wombles. 'The Watcher', written by Lemmy, was the closing track on Hawkwind's 1972 album *Doremi Fasol Latido*.

Joe Muggs of *theartsdesk.com* on 15 September 2018:

> Implausible times call for implausible music, and it doesn't come much more unlikely than this. Batt has removed all of the dirt, grease, diesel fumes, sticky bong residue and guitar distortion from the band's sound – this is a full-on showbiz spectacular, ballroom dance rhythms, big band brass, orchestral swoops and all.

Hawkwind's longest-serving member Dave Brock had been friends with Eric Clapton since the early 1960s, as he told *The Quietus*:

> In the early days I used to play blues guitar and Eric didn't have a guitar. We used to sit there and I would show a few chords to him, 'off you go' and then he'd have his guitar; we used to sit there playing together. I've got some photographs from then.

'The Watcher' is a bizarre one-note electro-blues, a phrase than can perhaps sum up Hawkwind's entire recorded output.

Ian Fortnam of *Loudersound* on 18 September 2018:

> The coup of securing Clapton's services for 'The Watcher' finds Slowhand sleepwalking through a masterclass in snoozy blues.

Perhaps more remarkably, Clapton joined Hawkwind on stage for eight songs at a show in Guildford in November 2019. Eric playing'Masters Of The Universe' and 'Silver Machine'? Yes, it really happened.

Doyle Bramhall II: ***Shades***

Recorded 2018 in Brooklyn, Austin, Jacksonville and Los Angeles. Released October 2018. Highest chart positions: did not chart. Produced by Doyle Bramhall II.

'Everything You Need (album version)' (Grace, Bramhall, Minkoff, Sherba)
'Everything You Need (single version)' (Grace, Bramhall, Minkoff, Sherba)
Clapton courted Doyle Bramhall II for years. They first worked together in 2000 during sessions for *Riding With The King*. Bramhall had turned heads after two well-received solo albums and as a member of Texan blues-rock band Arc Angels. He has added guitar (and sometimes original songs) to *Reptile* (2001), *Me and Mr. Johnson* (2004), *Sessions for Robert J* (2004), *Back Home* (2005), *The Road to Escondido* (2006), *Clapton* (2010), *Old Sock* (2013), *The Breeze: An Appreciation Of J. J. Cale* (2014) and *Happy Xmas* (2018). Bramhall has been a regular member of Clapton's live band since 2004. He wasn't yet born at the time of Cream's farewell concerts, but his pedigree is impeccable: his father, Doyle Bramhall had played in bands with Jimmie and Stevie Ray Vaughan in the late sixties and early seventies. Doyle, to *Guitarworld.com* in 2018:

> Jimmie and Stevie both impacted me in so many ways that shaped me as the guitar player and person I am today. They were my first and biggest influences — other than my father. Stevie always cared so much about what I was up to as a musician and about championing me. He would always ask me to show him my music and any songs I had written. He gave me the confidence to believe in myself and my music.

Shades is Bramhall's fifth solo album. 'Everything You Need' is a moody, slow-burning, funky soul/blues. Eric plays his trademark fills and adds two short, piercing solos against Bramhall's wah-wah rhythm. Bramhall:

> I just thought Eric would really like that song, knowing his taste and the things he's into. I thought it might catch his attention. And it's always nice to have

somebody that is a guest on a song that you think they might relate to or enjoy rather than just getting them on something they have no connection to at all. It was just a guess that he would like the track, and he did. Then he was in the US, and I just drove out to where he was recording and spent the day with him. The track wasn't even finished. I didn't have lyrics for it. I just had the basic tracks: drums, bass and a couple of guitars. Then I sang a melodic vocal idea, just so he'd know where to play, and all the gaps between that he could play in. And bam, he played it, and it sounded great.

The shorter single edit removes Eric's solo, but he can still be heard playing fills and unmistakably closing out the song with Bramhall's co-lead.

Sheryl Crow: *Threads*
Recorded 2016–2019 in Austin, Los Angeles, Chicago, Nashville and Burbank. Released 30 August 2019. Highest chart positions: UK: 10, US: 30. Produced by Steve Jordan, Sheryl Crow and Jeff Trott.

'Beware of Darkness' (Harrison)
Threads is an excellent duets album with some heavyweight pitchers: Stevie Nicks, Bonnie Raitt, Mavis Staples, Sting, Johnny Cash, Neil Young, Keith Richards, Willie Nelson, Kris Kristofferson, Joe Walsh, Emmylou Harris, James Taylor, Vince Gill and others.

Eric adds liquid lead guitar to Sheryl Crow's delicate reworking of one of George Harrison's best songs. Vocals are by Crow, Sting and Brandi Carlisle.

Pedrito Martinez: *Acertijos*
Recorded 2020 in London and Cuba. Released March 2021. Highest chart positions: did not chart. Produced by Pedrito Martinez.

'Aumba' (Martinez)
'My Father's Eyes' (Clapton)
'Yo Si Quiero' (Delgado Jr, Delgado, Martinez)
Pedro Pablo 'Pedrito' Martinez was born in 1973 in Havana and began his musical career at the age of eleven. Since settling in New York City in 1998, Pedrito has recorded or performed with Wynton Marsalis, Paul Simon, Paquito D'Rivera, Chucho Valdez, Bruce Springsteen, Eddie Palmieri, Dave Matthews, Jackson Browne, Elton John and Sting, and has contributed to well over one hundred albums.

Eric adds some flamenco-style acoustic guitar to 'Aumba', a percussion-heavy Cuban song. A re-recording of Clapton's 'My Father's Eyes' sees Clapton and Martinez sharing strong lead vocals. They had performed this together at the 2019 Crossroads Guitar Festival. The busy arrangement almost swamps the melody. 'Yo Si Quiero' is a funky jazz tune first released as a single in June 2020. It has Kenny Garrett on saxophone and Eric blasting a mean, dirty solo.

Epilogue

The two-hundred-plus extra-curricular projects listed here represent fifty years of guest sessions, both in the studio and in concert. This is a significant body of work to which few can compare.

With Clapton semi-retired, further sessions are likely to be small in number. But, surely, as long as he can pick up a guitar, he'll be ready to add a lick, riff or solo to anyone who asks him.

And more power to him for that.

Thanks Eric.

Eric's Greatest Hit Sessions

Eric Clapton has guested on twelve albums by others that have reached number one either in the US or UK (or both). In order of release they are:

The Beatles: *The Beatles*	US: 1	UK: 1
George Harrison: *All Things Must Pass*	US: 1	UK: 1
George Harrison and Friends: *The Concert For Bangladesh*	US: 2	UK: 1
Bob Dylan: *Desire*	US: 1	UK: 3
Phil Collins: *Face Value*	US: 7	UK: 1
Lionel Richie: *Dancing On The Ceiling*	US: 1	UK: 2
Sting: *...Nothing Like The Sun*	US: 9	UK: 1
Phil Collins: *But Seriously...*	US: 1	UK: 1
Santana: *Supernatural*	US: 1	UK: 1
Rod Stewart: *Stardust – The Great American Songbook Vol 3*	US: 1	UK: 3
The Rolling Stones: *Blue And Lonesome*	US: 4	UK: 1
Ed Sheeran: *Divide*	US: 1	UK: 1

Other US Top Ten Albums by Chart Placings

Aretha Franklin: *Lady Soul*	US: 2
The Who: *Tommy Original Soundtrack Recording*	US: 2
Mary J. Blige: *Mary*	US: 2
Stephen Stills: *Stephen Stills*	US: 3
Tina Turner: *Break Every Rule*	US: 4
The Rolling Stones: *Sticky Fingers* (2015 reissue)	US: 5
Paul McCartney: *Kisses On The Bottom*	US: 5
Babyface: *The Day*	US: 6
Stephen Stills: *Stephen Stills 2*	US: 8
George Harrison: *Cloud Nine*	US: 8

Other UK Top Ten Albums by Chart Placings

Tina Turner: *Break Every Rule*	UK: 2
Kate Bush: *The Red Shoes*	UK: 2
Kate Bush: *The Director's Cut*	UK: 2
Paul McCartney: *Kisses On The Bottom*	UK: 2
Eternal: *Before The Rain*	UK: 3
Mary J. Blige: *Mary*	UK: 5
The Rolling Stones: *Flashpoint*	UK: 6
The Rolling Stones: *Sticky Fingers* (2015 reissue)	UK: 7
Stephen Stills: *Stephen Stills*	UK: 8
Tina Turner: *Live In Europe*	UK: 8
Cyndi Lauper: *A Night To Remember*	UK: 9
George Harrison: *Cloud Nine*	UK: 10
Sheryl Crow: *Threads*	UK: 10

Bibliography

Badman, K., *The Beatles Diary Volume 2: After the Break-Up 1970–2001* (Omnibus Press, London, 2001)

Bowling, D., *Eric Clapton FAQ* (Backbeat Books, Milwaukee, 2013)

Clapton, E., *Eric Clapton: The Autobiography* (Broadway, New York, 2007)

Coleman, R., *Survivor – The Authorized biography of Eric Clapton* (Futura Publications, London, 1986)

Collins, P., *Not Dead Yet: The Autobiography* (Century St. Albans, 2016)

Christgau, R., *Christgau's Guide: Rock Albums of the Seventies* (Vermilion, London, 1982)

Ewbank, T. and Hildred, S., *Roger Daltrey The Biography* (Piatkus, London, 2012)

Frame, P. *Rock Family Trees* (Omnibus Press, London, 1980)

Hammack, J., *The Beatles Recording Reference Manual Volume 4 (1968-early 1969)* (Gearfab, Toronto, 2020)

Heylin, C. *Bob Dylan. The Recording Sessions [1960 – 1994]* (St. Martin's Press. London, 1995)

Johns, G., *Sound Man : A Life Recording Hits with the Rolling Stones, The Who, Led Zeppelin, The Eagles, Eric Clapton, The Faces.* (Plume, New York, 2015)

Kruppa, J. and Womack, K., *All Things Must Pass Away* (Chicago Review Press, Chicago, 2021)

Lauper, C. and Dunn, J., A Memoir (Simon & Schuster, London, 2013)

Lewisohn, M., *The Complete Beatles Recording Sessions: The Official Story of the Abbey Road Years 1962-1970* (Hamlyn, London, 1988)

Madinger, C., and Easter, M., *Eight Arms to Hold You: The Solo Beatles Compendium* (44 1 Productions Inc, Chesterfield MO, 2001)

Norman P., *Slowhand: The Life and Music of Eric Clapton* (W&N, London, 2018)

Quinonero, F., *Françoise Hardy, un long chant d'amour* (L'Archipel, Amsterdam, 2017)

Robertson, R., *Testimony* (Crown Archetype, London, 2016)

Roberty, M., *Eric Clapton – The New Visual Documentary* (Omnibus Press, London, 1990)

In his own words – Eric Clapton (Omnibus Press, London, 1993)

Eric Clapton – The Complete Recording Sessions 1963-1992 (Blandford, London, 1993)

The Eric Clapton Scrapbook (Citadel Press, New York, 1994)

Eric Clapton – The Complete Guide to His Music (Omnibus Press, London, 2005)

Shapiro, H., *Eric Clapton – Lost In The Blues* (Da Capo, Boston, 1992)

Tisserand. M., *The Kingdom Of Zydeco* (Arcade Publishing, New York, 1998)

Townshend, P., *Who I Am* (HarperCollins, 2012)

Whitlock, B. with Roberty, M., *A Rock 'n' Roll Autobiography* (McFarland & Co., Jefferson, 2010)

Winn, J.C., *That Magic Feeling: The Beatles' Recorded Legacy, Volume Two, 1966-1970* (Random House, Woodland Hills, 2009)

On Track series

Alan Parsons Project – Steve Swift 978-1-78952-154-2
Tori Amos – Lisa Torem 978-1-78952-142-9
Asia – Peter Braidis 978-1-78952-099-6
Badfinger – Robert Day-Webb 978-1-878952-176-4
Barclay James Harvest – Keith and Monica Domone 978-1-78952-067-5
The Beatles – Andrew Wild 978-1-78952-009-5
The Beatles Solo 1969-1980 – Andrew Wild 978-1-78952-030-9
Blue Oyster Cult – Jacob Holm-Lupo 978-1-78952-007-1
Blur – Matt Bishop 978-178952-164-1
Marc Bolan and T.Rex – Peter Gallagher 978-1-78952-124-5
Kate Bush – Bill Thomas 978-1-78952-097-2
Camel – Hamish Kuzminski 978-1-78952-040-8
Caravan – Andy Boot 978-1-78952-127-6
Cardiacs – Eric Benac 978-1-78952-131-3
Eric Clapton Solo – Andrew Wild 978-1-78952-141-2
The Clash – Nick Assirati 978-1-78952-077-4
Crosby, Stills and Nash – Andrew Wild 978-1-78952-039-2
The Damned – Morgan Brown 978-1-78952-136-8
Deep Purple and Rainbow 1968-79 – Steve Pilkington 978-1-78952-002-6
Dire Straits – Andrew Wild 978-1-78952-044-6
The Doors – Tony Thompson 978-1-78952-137-5
Dream Theater – Jordan Blum 978-1-78952-050-7
Electric Light Orchestra – Barry Delve 978-1-78952-152-8
Elvis Costello and The Attractions – Georg Purvis 978-1-78952-129-0
Emerson Lake and Palmer – Mike Goode 978-1-78952-000-2
Fairport Convention – Kevan Furbank 978-1-78952-051-4
Peter Gabriel – Graeme Scarfe 978-1-78952-138-2
Genesis – Stuart MacFarlane 978-1-78952-005-7
Gentle Giant – Gary Steel 978-1-78952-058-3
Gong – Kevan Furbank 978-1-78952-082-8
Hall and Oates – Ian Abrahams 978-1-78952-167-2
Hawkwind – Duncan Harris 978-1-78952-052-1
Peter Hammill – Richard Rees Jones 978-1-78952-163-4
Roy Harper – Opher Goodwin 978-1-78952-130-6
Jimi Hendrix – Emma Stott 978-1-78952-175-7
The Hollies – Andrew Darlington 978-1-78952-159-7
Iron Maiden – Steve Pilkington 978-1-78952-061-3
Jefferson Airplane – Richard Butterworth 978-1-78952-143-6
Jethro Tull – Jordan Blum 978-1-78952-016-3
Elton John in the 1970s – Peter Kearns 978-1-78952-034-7

The Incredible String Band – Tim Moon 978-1-78952-107-8
Iron Maiden – Steve Pilkington 978-1-78952-061-3
Judas Priest – John Tucker 978-1-78952-018-7
Kansas – Kevin Cummings 978-1-78952-057-6
The Kinks – Martin Hutchinson 978-1-78952-172-6
Korn – Matt Karpe 978-1-78952-153-5
Led Zeppelin – Steve Pilkington 978-1-78952-151-1
Level 42 – Matt Philips 978-1-78952-102-3
Little Feat – 978-1-78952-168-9
Aimee Mann – Jez Rowden 978-1-78952-036-1
Joni Mitchell – Peter Kearns 978-1-78952-081-1
The Moody Blues – Geoffrey Feakes 978-1-78952-042-2
Motorhead – Duncan Harris 978-1-78952-173-3
Mike Oldfield – Ryan Yard 978-1-78952-060-6
Opeth – Jordan Blum 978-1-78-952-166-5
Tom Petty – Richard James 978-1-78952-128-3
Porcupine Tree – Nick Holmes 978-1-78952-144-3
Queen – Andrew Wild 978-1-78952-003-3
Radiohead – William Allen 978-1-78952-149-8
Renaissance – David Detmer 978-1-78952-062-0
The Rolling Stones 1963-80 – Steve Pilkington 978-1-78952-017-0
The Smiths and Morrissey – Tommy Gunnarsson 978-1-78952-140-5
Status Quo the Frantic Four Years – Richard James 978-1-78952-160-3
Steely Dan – Jez Rowden 978-1-78952-043-9
Steve Hackett – Geoffrey Feakes 978-1-78952-098-9
Thin Lizzy – Graeme Stroud 978-1-78952-064-4
Toto – Jacob Holm-Lupo 978-1-78952-019-4
U2 – Eoghan Lyng 978-1-78952-078-1
UFO – Richard James 978-1-78952-073-6
The Who – Geoffrey Feakes 978-1-78952-076-7
Roy Wood and the Move – James R Turner 978-1-78952-008-8
Van Der Graaf Generator – Dan Coffey 978-1-78952-031-6
Yes – Stephen Lambe 978-1-78952-001-9
Frank Zappa 1966 to 1979 – Eric Benac 978-1-78952-033-0
Warren Zevon – Peter Gallagher 978-1-78952-170-2
10CC – Peter Kearns 978-1-78952-054-5

Decades Series

The Bee Gees in the 1960s – Andrew Mon Hughes et al 978-1-78952-148-1
The Bee Gees in the 1970s – Andrew Mon Hughes et al 978-1-78952-179-5
Black Sabbath in the 1970s – Chris Sutton 978-1-78952-171-9
Britpop – Peter Richard Adams and Matt Pooler 978-1-78952-169-6

Alice Cooper in the 1970s – Chris Sutton 978-1-78952-104-7
Curved Air in the 1970s – Laura Shenton 978-1-78952-069-9
Bob Dylan in the 1980s – Don Klees 978-1-78952-157-3
Fleetwood Mac in the 1970s – Andrew Wild 978-1-78952-105-4
Focus in the 1970s – Stephen Lambe 978-1-78952-079-8
Free and Bad Company in the 1970s – John Van der Kiste 978-1-78952-178-8
Genesis in the 1970s – Bill Thomas 978178952-146-7
George Harrison in the 1970s – Eoghan Lyng 978-1-78952-174-0
Marillion in the 1980s – Nathaniel Webb 978-1-78952-065-1
Mott the Hoople and Ian Hunter in the 1970s – John Van der Kiste 978-1-78-952-162-7
Pink Floyd In The 1970s – Georg Purvis 978-1-78952-072-9
Tangerine Dream in the 1970s – Stephen Palmer 978-1-78952-161-0
The Sweet in the 1970s – Darren Johnson 978-1-78952-139-9
Uriah Heep in the 1970s – Steve Pilkington 978-1-78952-103-0
Yes in the 1980s – Stephen Lambe with David Watkinson 978-1-78952-125-2

On Screen series

Carry On… – Stephen Lambe 978-1-78952-004-0
David Cronenberg – Patrick Chapman 978-1-78952-071-2
Doctor Who: The David Tennant Years – Jamie Hailstone 978-1-78952-066-8
James Bond – Andrew Wild – 978-1-78952-010-1
Monty Python – Steve Pilkington 978-1-78952-047-7
Seinfeld Seasons 1 to 5 – Stephen Lambe 978-1-78952-012-5

Other Books

1967: A Year In Psychedelic Rock – Kevan Furbank 978-1-78952-155-9
1970: A Year In Rock – John Van der Kiste 978-1-78952-147-4
1973: The Golden Year of Progressive Rock – Geoffrey Feakes 978-1-78952-165-8
Babysitting A Band On The Rocks – G.D. Praetorius 978-1-78952-106-1
Eric Clapton Sessions – Andrew Wild 978-1-78952-177-1
Derek Taylor: For Your Radioactive Children – Andrew Darlington 978-1-78952-038-5
The Golden Road: The Recording History of The Grateful Dead – John Kilbride 978-1-78952-156-6
Iggy and The Stooges On Stage 1967-1974 – Per Nilsen 978-1-78952-101-6
Jon Anderson and the Warriors – the road to Yes – David Watkinson 978-1-78952-059-0
Nu Metal: A Definitive Guide – Matt Karpe 978-1-78952-063-7
Tommy Bolin: In and Out of Deep Purple – Laura Shenton 978-1-78952-070-5
Maximum Darkness – Deke Leonard 978-1-78952-048-4
Maybe I Should've Stayed In Bed – Deke Leonard 978-1-78952-053-8
The Twang Dynasty – Deke Leonard 978-1-78952-049-1

and many more to come!

Would you like to write for Sonicbond Publishing?

We are mainly a music publisher, but we also occasionally publish in other genres including film and television. At Sonicbond Publishing we are always on the look-out for authors, particularly for our two main series, On Track and Decades.

Mixing fact with in depth analysis, the On Track series examines the entire recorded work of a particular musical artist or group. All genres are considered from easy listening and jazz to 60s soul to 90s pop, via rock and metal.

The Decades series singles out a particular decade in an artist or group's history and focuses on that decade in more detail than may be allowed in the On Track series.

While professional writing experience would, of course, be an advantage, the most important qualification is to have real enthusiasm and knowledge of your subject. First-time authors are welcomed, but the ability to write well in English is essential.

Sonicbond Publishing has distribution throughout Europe and North America, and all our books are also published in E-book form. Authors will be paid a royalty based on sales of their book. Further details about our books are available from www.sonicbondpublishing.com. To contact us, complete the contact form there or email info@sonicbondpublishing.co.uk